Laughton Osborn

The Montanini

The School for Critics

Laughton Osborn

The Montanini
The School for Critics

ISBN/EAN: 9783337375942

Printed in Europe, USA, Canada, Australia, Japan

Cover: Foto ©Andreas Hilbeck / pixelio.de

More available books at **www.hansebooks.com**

THE MONTANINI

THE SCHOOL FOR CRITICS

COMEDIES

BEING IN CONTINUATION AND COMPLETION
OF THE FOURTH VOLUME OF THE DRAMATIC SERIES

BY

LAUGHTON OSBORN

NEW YORK
JAMES MILLER, 647 BROADWAY
MDCCCLXVIII

THE NEW YORK PRINTING COMPANY,
81, 83, and 85 Centre St.,
NEW YORK.

THE MONTANINI'

MDCCCLVI

CHARACTERS, ETC.

CARLO DI TOMMA'SO MONTANINO,[2] ⎱ *Young nobles*
IPPOL'ITO DE' SALIMBENI,[3]　　　 ⎰　*of rival families.*
GAS'PARO BECCARI, *one of the Nine Magistrates of the City.*
GIAC'OMO GRADENATA, *a citizen of honorable but decayed family.*

GIANNI, *aged servant of Carlo.*
ANTONELLO, *servant of Ippolito.*
Captain of Sbirri.

ANGELICA, *Carlo's sister.*
CORNELIA, *Ippolito's sister.*
DOMICILLA, *his maiden aunt.*
CAMILLA VOLPICINA[4], *a widow, sister of Giacomo.*
BARBARA, *Angelica's maid.*

　　　　　　Mute Persons.
SBIRRI.　A JAILER.

———

SCENE. *In Siena, in the Y.* 1322.

THE MONTANINI

ACT THE FIRST

SCENE I. *In the Palazzo Montanini.*

CARLO. ANGELICA. BECCARI.

Carlo. I have said enough, Ser Gasparo Beccari.[b]
    You cannot have the farm.
                Becc. Well, make it ten.
A thousand golden florins is a price
None but myself would offer.   Need I say,
'Tis solely that our two estates adjoin,
I bid so largely ?
        Carlo. But you bid in vain :
It is my sole possession, save this house.
And knowing this much I wonder you should strive
To oust me from it.
         Becc. Messer Montanino,

You will perhaps not easily lend belief,
That I, of the vulgar people who have driven
Your overbearing order from the State,
And who, being of the people, have been made
One of their magistrates, thus bound to see
That such of you as we suffer to remain
Lift not their heads in the city, to o'erride it
And bring again the rule of noble blood
And servile vassalage of poor to rich,—
You 'll not believe that I, being such, should feel ——
I weary you perhaps, or chafe?

     Carlo. Not either.
My humble fortune teaches me to bear;
Nor was I born impatient.

     Becc. That, I say,
Being what I am, I have charity for you
A noble of old blood, you will not credit.
But I am Christian more than in my faith,
And hold all men my brothers. When I think
How great your sires, how wealthy, and how proud,
Whose arms are everywhere — on palace-gate
And castle-tower, yet all of which have pass'd
To other, and to mostly meaner hands,
As you would deem them ——

     Carlo. 'Twas my sires' own fault.
Becc. Truly. They wasted upon private feuds
 The blood and treasure should have serv'd the State.
Carlo. Pass over that. You do not keep me here
 To tell me that my ancestors were fools?

Becc. I do not keep you here, I hope, at all.

That I am come, is even for what I said.

Shall I have license to explain myself?

When I consider all your glorious past,

And see what you are now: these palace-walls,

Wherein might dwell a hundred cavaliers

Nor yet be crowded, cheerless now and bare,

Without perhaps one chamber meetly furnish'd

For such a presence as your lady-sister's ——

[*his eyes, which have glanced around the room with half-covert mockery, now resting with open admiration on Angelica.*

Carlo. Messer Beccari! does your Christian heart

Bid you insult my ——

Becc. Poverty? Now Heaven

Give you more insight, and make known your friends!

My Christian heart, Messere Montanino,

Bids me have pity both of you and yours.

I find you living in this stately house

Straighten'd by indigence, with means sufficient

Scarcely to keep yourselves, and one small maid,

And an old porter, safe from winter's cold.

I offer for your farm a liberal price,

Which properly invested would enlarge

Your narrow income: and to show I act

With a pure sympathy for you, and yours,

[*looking again at Angelica.*

Make now the ten twelve hundred. If the farm

Is pretty, it is small.

Carlo. But large enough,
To give me here that living which, if mean,
I not complain of, certainly not to you.
Messer Beccari, it may be — I hope
Truly it is — that you are well my friend.
So rest: but give me leave to plainly tell you,
My enemy Salimbene would not speak
With such disparagement.   If my fallen estate
Touch you with sympathy, keep it in your breast.
'T is friendship to alleviate distress ;
But to remind the sufferer of his wo
Looks more like malice.

                  Becc. Heaven is my judge,
I meant it well.   I pray you be not blind.
For your sweet sister's sake, subdue this pride.
Will you nöt make provision for a future
So rich in promise, as hers must be whose present
Is full of grace ? [*again looking admiringly on Angelica.*
         Carlo. [*with some asperity, but without passion.*
       Ser Gasparo Beccari,
You can, I think, find out your way alone.
I have but one male servant, as you said,
And he is old.

     With a slight and distant inclination, but without
       disdain, CARLO, *putting through his own the*
         arm of ANGELICA, *who, for the greater*
          part of the dialogue, has stood lean-
           ing with her left hand on Carlo's
            right shoulder, leads her out.

Becc. [*with a low, but deep utterance.*

The devil take thy pride,
Thou last green scion of a blasted tree ! —
But she ! How dark this desolate house appears
Now she is vanish'd ! With what grace she lean'd
On her stiff brother ! Not the fairest form
Of all the yellow marbles of old Greece,
Not the most delicate of the dainty Three
Men call the Graces, which my father's day
Saw disinterr'd where stand the Duomo's walls,°
Has such an attitude. Ah ! could I gain her !
And ruin him ! — Perhaps, to ruin him
Would be to gain her. She adores the beggar,
And would do aught to save him. — Let me think.
       [*Exit—pensively.*

Scene II.

In the house of Giacomo.

Giacomo. Camilla.

Giac. Yes, that I do ! By Paul ! I doubt him much.
 Beccari is but fooling thee.
    Camil. Fooling *me?*
Giac. Yea, thee, Camilla Widow Volpicina.

Is that impossible, I should like to know?

Camil. Giacomo Bachelor Gradenata, ay;
   If that thou mean'st that Gasparo Beccari,
   Were he twice the man he is, could cozen me,
   And I not know it. But thou dost him wrong.
   He loves me, and ——

                   Giac. Why don't he wed thee then?
   Since he first woo'd thee, it is now two years.
   He does not wait for either to grow old.

Camil. No, nor grow young: we both are young enough,
   And can afford to dally. 'Tis so sweet
   The hour of courtship that I wonder not
   Men should prolong it; and for me, I care not
   To hasten on the time when I must cease
   To rule as mistress and be rul'd as slave.

Giac. That 's talk for a widow, now! By holy Paul!
   I don't believe a word of it! Tell me truly;
   Dost thou love Gasparo then?

                   Camil. My brother, yes.
   Else would I wed him?

                   Giac. [*laughing harshly.*
                   What a fox thou art!
   But I am not a goose. A loving widow,
   And like long courtships! Thou 'rt a jet-black swan.
   Dost thou forget, my sentimental sister,
   That we are poor, and Gasparo the rich
   May fancy some one who is more his mate?
   He 's a republican, and upholds, thou knowest,
   A pure equality.

Camil. Sorrow on thy jests !
They are like the eye of a serpent : and thy laugh
Is pleasant as its hiss.

    Giac. Meek-thoughted sister !

Camil. Thou art a friend of Gasparo's. —

      Giac. Ay, his friend.
And he is mine : I use him. But I do
Distrust him damnably. I wish he 'd wed thee.

Camil. And so he will. What is the match to thee ?

Giac. 'Twould leave one weight the less upon my mind,
And make at least one Gradenata rich.
Thou knowest thy charms : it is not I, that bill
And coo with Gasparo : but he 'll jilt thee, see !
For thou art poor.

    Camil. And he is rich for both.
Besides, I bring him what he lacks.

      Giac. What 's that ?
Long hair and beardless lips ?

      Camil. What most he prizes : ·
Good birth and stainless lineage. If I stoop'd
To wed the notary Batto Volpicina,
I shall not raise the Gradenate high
By looking on a butcher's son.

      Giac. He 's here.

Enter BECCARI.

Becc. What, my·fair Volscian, though not Dian's nymph.'
He takes her hand, though somewhat constrainedly.

Camil. [*As he holds her hands,*

   looking intently in his eyes.   (*He looks aside.*)

I am glad to see thee, Gasparo; but I fear,

Thou art not well to-day.

      Becc. Why so?   Not well?

Camil. Or art not glad to see me in thy turn.

Becc. Poh, child! that is but fancy.   Yet I am

In sooth disturb'd: a slight affair gone wrong —

The business of the State ——

    [*looks at Giacomo significantly, then at Camilla,*

     and at the door (*not unobserved by Camilla*).

       Thy brother and I

Will talk it over.

    Giac. Camilla, for awhile,

Leave us alone.

    Camil. I hope thy brow will clear

By my return, dear Gasparo; but methinks

Thou'lt find poor help for business of the State

In Giacomo's unus'd brain. [*going up.*

      Becc. O, 'tis not much —

A small affair, I said. [*Exit Camil. by a door above — turn-*

    ing round and smiling on Becc. as she disappears.

  BECCARI *and* GIACOMO *bring down chairs.*

[*First looking round at the door.*]   How goes it with thee?

Has thy luck turn'd, my friend?

      Giac. By Bacchus! no!

I'm devilishly us'd up.   I hope, Beccari,

Thou wilt not soon be asking for thy gold?

Becc. No, I would rather lend thee twice as much,
　　So thou might'st win that back.　But truly, Giacomo,
　　Thou 'rt a sad spendthrift; and I dread to think,
　　What with thy dice and women, thou mayst come
　　One day to ruin.
　　　　　Giac. No, I know my verge:
　　I shall stop short of it.　But 'tis not spending
　　Too fast or much, but little, keeps me down.
　　Just when my luck is turning, lo, I stop!
　　For want of more to venture.　Cursed fate!
Becc. What was thy last loss?
　　　　　　Giac. Five and twenty florins.
　　Pio Birban'te offer'd me revenge.
　　I could not take it; and he laugh'd, pest on him!
Becc. Thou think'st thou couldst have won again?
　　　　　　　　Giac. Am sure.
　　Thus stood the game: I'll show thee how. —
　　　　　　　Becc. No matter.
　　Thou'dst like again to venture?[8]
　　　　　　　Giac. But I shame
　　Again to ask thee, Gasparo.
　　　　　　Becc. Poh! shame not.
　　Shall we not soon be brothers?　Let me see.
　　Now, I will venture four times twenty-five,
　　And double that, so thou wilt do for me
　　Something in turn.
　　　　　Giac. [*suspiciously.*
　　　　　Eh!　'T is some mischief.
　　　　　　　　Becc. Fi!

　　　12*

Thy old distrust!   How prompt thou art to borrow,
But slow to lend!

     Giac. [*starting up.*⁹

    Come, Gasparo Beccari,
This is too much!   I am not, man, thy slave.

Becc. No, but thou art thy passions'.   Look thou now!
What a poor wayward, tetchy thing thou art!
Suspecting me; but, when I in return
Tax thee with scanty kindness ——

       Giac. By St. John!
Thou didst reproach me —— Blisters on my tongue!
I shame to mention it.

      Becc. Thou hast no cause.
Come, set thee down.   I say — thou hast no cause.¹⁰
I had no thought of money.   And if I had,
Are we not brothers?   Thou wouldst do for me
As much, were my lot thine.   I wish it were.¹¹

Giac. Well, that is kindly.   I will take thy offer.
I 'll try my luck once more, and then leave off
When I have won enough.

     Becc. Why, that is wise.

Giac. [*again suspiciously.*
  Thou mockest.

     Becc. On my soul! —— But only try
Largely.   I 'll back thee, till thou hast made thyself.

Giac. Wilt thou? [*seizing his hand.*
    That's brave!   But what is to be done?
By Jupiter! this much will call for much,
Or I mistake thee.   'T is the state-affair;

Eh, my Beccari?

        Becc. Psha! that was a blind.

Camilla has sharp eyes.[12]

                Thou knowest, I think,

How I have long'd to buy that little farm

In the sweet vale of Strove, next my own.

The beggar Montanino ——

            Giac. Speak more low;

Camilla has quick ears.[13]

           Becc. 'T is well reminded.

What was that noise?   Come out, to the open air.

Close walls are not for secrets.   [*Exit, leading out Giac.*

           Camil. [*coming in from the door.*

              Say'st thou so?

Why so it is then.   Thou hast stopp'd my ears.

I hardly think thou 'lt put out both my eyes.

One is for Giacomo. —   [*Pondering.*]   Montanino, eh? —

And thou hast long'd to buy his little farm? —

He 'll not then sell it. —   And my brother brib'd

Through his pernicious vice. —   Here is some plot.

Ah ha!   And thou a magistrate!   'T is well.

I 'll be at the bottom of this before thou knowest.

Then try to shake me from thee, an' thou dare!

Thou think'st I love thee.   I should love to be

The mistress of thy household.   And I will.

      Goes up the stage again, towards the door:

            and Scene closes.

Scene III.

*The Piazza del Campo
with the Fonte Gaja.*
Barbara
*is seen dipping a terra-cotta pitcher of antique form into
the Fountain. She raises it to her head, when
Enter, from the left,*
Antonello.
*Barbara going off to the right as Antonello crosses the stage,
she looks half-aside, and pretends to hurry from
him. He arrests her.*

Anton. Eh, barbarous Barbara! whither off so fast?
    Don't our ways lie together? Stop a little!
    Nobody's looking. There. [*looking about him,*
                            snatches a kiss.
                    Thou 'rt quite a blossom!
Barb. If our ways lie together, saucy Nello,
    Yet our two houses, please, stand quite apart.
    The Montanini [*affecting grandeur*] have no consort with
    The Salimbeni.
        Anton. Better if they had.
Barb. Come, that's a deal too impudent. Dost think,
    Because we are poor, we 're not as proud as you?
    I have seen thy master look prodigious sweet

On my sweet mistress.

        Anton. Hast thou ? So have I.

Would n't it be a blessing, eh ! My lord —

Thy lady — eh ? The Palace in a blaze ——

Barb. A blessing that ! — There 's little though to burn.

                      [shrugging her shoulders.

Anton. I meant a blaze of lights, and not of fire.

They two made one, my little maid and I

Might hunt in couples. Eh, my dainty rib ! *[pinching her.*

Barb. Ouf ! Don't now ! Get away ! thou 'lt make me spill

My water. And — *[looking off the scene.*

            St. Domenic ! get thee gone !

There 's Gianni coming ! Do go, Nello dear !

Anton. Kiss me then, first.

            Barb. Not I !

                Anton. I sha' n't go then ;

Nor shalt thou either.

            Barb. *[struggling and looking*

                off the scene.

            Patience ! — There ! *[kissing him.*

                    And there !

                [striking him on the ear.

Anton. *[laughing and rubbing his ear.*

    I 'll pay thee, Monna Barbara !

            Exit, at the right,

while Enter from the same, passing him, GIANNI.

            Gian. *[looking at him discontentedly*

                and shaking his head.

            So — so — so !

Always with Antonello.   I 'm a-thinking,
Thou 'dst best have nought to do with Master's foes.
That 's my idea!

    Barb. He is n't Master's foe.
Nor is his master either.

     Gian. I say he is.
They have been foes for twice a hundred years.
Now!   And I 'm thinking, thou hadst best come home
At once.   That 's my idea.

     Barb. And my idea
Is, thou hadst better mind thy own affairs.
Gian. I am a-minding of my own affairs.
The Mistress sent for thee.

     Barb. Why couldst thou not
Say that at once? [*hurrying off to right.*

   Enter BECCARI, *from left,*
    and stops her.

  Becc. My pretty Barbara!   What!
Both out together!   How will the old house
Do without one of you?

    Gian. 'T is n't an old house;
And 't will do very well without, I 'm thinking,
If Master will it.   Come away. [*to Barb.*]   Thou 'dst best
Have nought to do with magistrates, I 'm thinking.
That 's my idea.   [*Exit, with Barb., at right.*

    Becc. And so 't is mine, old fellow.
Pointing after them
 scoffingly.]   A goodly retinue for a noble house!

Thou 'lt manage, though, to do without even these,
I 'm thinking [*mimicking Gianni*], Messer Carlo.

                                       All is ready.

In a few minutes! —— 'T was a hard ado
To bring my would-be brother to the mark.
I bad him high. He 'd sell his soul to the Devil
For means to game with. Even such fools does vice,
When grown a habit, make of men ! — I 'll walk
About this place, until the work be done,
And glut my soul with that proud beggar's shame.

    He looks down the street where Barbara, &c.,
             had disappeared, and
               Scene closes.

Scene IV.

In the Palazzo Montanini. Angelica's Apartment.
Angelica *seated embroidering.*
Carlo *stands behind her, looking abstractedly on her work.*
After a few moments,

Carlo. Angelica — I cannot drive from mind   .
    That man's presumption. And it wakens now —
    What memory, think'st thou ? — Salimbene's looks
    Bent on my sister with such fond regard.

Angel. [confused, and bending low over her work,
which she discontinues.

   Oh Carlo! thou wouldst not compare the two?
Carlo. Now God forbid! I would not be unjust
   Even to an enemy. Leave thy work awhile.

They come forward.
He puts his right arm round her waist, and
takes her left hand in his left.

Now tell me, sweet: has Salimbene ever
Given token of a wish to come more near?
Angel. [with eyes cast down.

   Never, my brother, more than thou hast seen.
When from my way to church with Barbara sole
He meets me passing, bowing reverent-low,
With head unbonneted, he yields the path
As any noble cavalier might do
To noble damsel of a neighboring house."—
Carlo. Even though an enemy's. And that is all?
Angel. And that is all.

        Carlo. And tak'st thou not, sweet sister,
More pleasure in his homage than in that
Of other noble cavalier?— Forgive me;
I have no right to call this color here. [*pressing his lips to*
                        her cheek.

But oh, forget not, that we stand alone,
And should be all in all to one another.
Angel. [throwing both her arms about him.

   And we are all in all to one another.

Carlo. [*after pressing her a moment to*
     his breast, lifts her off, and resumes.

    And being alone should watch with double care
    That not a stain come on our father's name.
    Be charier of thy smiles to Salimbene.

Angel. I have not been more than courteous that I know;
    At least, I have never thought to be. Oh why,
    Why, brother, lend thy bosom to distrust?
    Ippolito Salimbene, all men say,
    Is open in heart as visage, and high-soul'd.

Carlo. Yet he is wealthy: we are very poor.

Angel. Does wealth exclude all virtue?

                 Carlo. No. But men
    Magnify into virtue in the rich
    All that is not bare vice; as in the poor
    The smallest spot of error swells to sin
    That is enormous. Salimbene's heart
    Has never felt misfortune. What should cloud
    His happy visage? Plac'd above dependance,
    He needs not feel distrust. So, says the world,
    " Behold a frank and generous-minded man ! "
    Perhaps he is. But I, being poor, if sad
    Am call'd morose; and if, for I have found
    In my adversity men cold and false,
    Slothful to help and eager to betray,
    I doubt and stand aloof, I am thought suspicious,
    And my reserve set down to gloomy pride.

Angel. Oh how they wrong thee, brother ! Let them come
    And ask of me. Thou art not proud, not gloomy;

Thou art thyself too generous and true,
To be suspicious of another's faith.
Carlo. Thou little flatterer! What canst thou know?
Art thou then of the kind which men suspect?
And to be gloomy under thy sweet smiles,
Why that, my sister, were as one should shiver
In the glad vernal sunshine. Thou art right:
I have no ague; not o' the heart at least.

Enter BARBARA.

But here is Barbara. Give her now her task,
And let us go.

ANGELICA *passes up the stage with* BARBARA, *and appears
to give directions about another piece of
embroidery, not her own.*

                    The air of this dull house
Even here, where it seems lightest, weighs us down.
What a rough nest for such a dainty bird! [*glancing
                    round him, and then fondly on
                    his sister's figure.*
I could for her sake almost see it chang'd
Even for an enemy's bower.

        ANGELICA, *leaving* BARBARA *at the frame,
        comes down.*

                Angel. What dost say,
Carlino?
    Carlo. I was murmuring at Heaven,

Which, when it made thee all an angel, sweet,
Forgot thy wings.

Angel. So I should fly away,
And leave thee lonely? Earth is good enough
With only thee, dear Carlo.

                * *Carlo.* Come then out.
The open air is better for us birds.
The heavens shall be our canopy; the turf
A more elastic footing than these boards;
The sunshine and the mottled shadows yield
All that we need to decorate our rooms,
Nor twit our poverty.

      Noise heard within, like the measured
        tramp of an armed band. ·

               What means that noise?

Enter GIANNI *in dismay.*

Gian. O my dear master! here's the guard broke in.
Carlo. What are they come for?

          Gian. For no good, I'm thinking.
I could not keep them off. Make haste! They're here!
Fly, Messer Carlo! hide yourself! O do!
Carlo. Not so. I must be found.

     ANGELICA *clings to her brother's arm.*
BARBARA, *who has already left her work, comes forward, as*

          Enter

  a party of SBIRRI, *headed by their* CAPTAIN.

         Whom seek ye here?

By whose command?

    Capt. By order of the Nine,
I come to arrest Ser Carlo Montanino,
Son of Messer' Tomma'so Montanino.
You are he, I think.

    Carlo. I am.　'T is some mistake.

Gian. 'T is some mean villany: that's my idea.

Carlo. Hush, good old man! — On what grounds is this done?

Capt. 'T is not my part to answer.　Lo, Messere,
You have my warrant.

    Unfolding it, and, bowing over the seal,
  he hands the parchment to CARLO, *who looks over it.*

    Carlo. I own it, and obey.

        [*returning the warrant.*

Angel. Oh no! he has done no wrong!　It cannot be!
O let him stay: you can confine him here.

Capt. Lady, it grieves me ——

    Carlo. Sister, be assur'd.
Do not cling to me so!　All will be well.
Once found their error, I shall soon be back.
Now there!　Now there!

    Angel. One moment! [*still clinging.*

      Carlo. Oh my heart!
'T is my sole terror, that I leave thee here,
Afflicted and alone.　Come then, bear up!
Wilt thou not for a little, for my sake?
There! [*kissing her*].　Take her, Barbara.　So.

      Now, Captain, quickly.

        [*hurrying off.*

Angel. Oh God! My brother! — Take me! take me too!

[*half-fainting in Carlo's arms.*

CARLO, *kissing her on the forehead, puts
her into the arms of* BARBARA, *and is led off, bending
his eyes continually on his sister.*

Drop falls.

ACT THE SECOND

SCENE I. *In the Palazzo Salimbeni.*

DOMICILLA. CORNELIA.

Cornel. No, Aunt, I cannot think it.   To be glad,
　　Ippolito should be spiteful.   Yet he is one
　　Of the best good-natur'd men in all Siena.
Domicil. And so he may be, yet be not ill pleas'd
　　His enemy is in prison.   In my day,
　　Men were good haters.   But the times are chang'd.
Cornel. Not in good hating, Aunt.   I am sure, if that
　　Be a sign of progress, manhood in our day
　　Is not degenerate.   The Tolome'i
　　And Salimbeni hate like Christians still.
Domicil. They are the heads of two great factions, child.
　　Why wilt thou contradict me?   In my day,
　　I say, men were not so.
　　　　　　　Cornel. I had no thought
　　To contradict thee, Aunt.
　　　　　　　Domicil. Now there, Cornelia!
　　Again thou contradictest.   In my day,
　　Men did not easily forget a wrong.
　　Thy brother, thou wilt see, despite his mirth,
　　Will find a serious pleasure in the shame

Of Carlo Montanino.

     Cornel. Poor young man !

What harm did he do my brother ?

        Domicil. How thou talk'st !

Are they not enemies ?

       Cornel. Their foresires were,

Some generations back.

       Domicil. Then so are they.

That is inevitable.

     Cornel. O dear Aunt!

Domicil. Why, is he not a friend of the Tolomei ?

Cornel. But then he is so poor ! what can he do ?

  Think of his desolation, all alone

  With one young sister; not another left

  Of all his father's house !

      Domicil. Whose fault is that?

  The sins of the fathers, child, are punish'd down

  To their fourth generation. 'T is the law

  Given out in thunder from the Mount of God.

Cornel. And writ in the code of Nature, but annull'd

  By later dispensation, in so far

  At least as mortal hands are made to wield

  The rod of Heaven's vengeance. We are told

  Not to take eye for eye and tooth for tooth,

  But lend two cheeks to the striker, and to him

  Who steals our cloak to give the mantle also.

Domicil. That may be preaching, child, but 'tis not practice.

  At least it was not so, when I was young.

Cornel. No, then it was taking all. Who filch'd your cloak,

Was sure to get the mantle, if he could.

Domicil. And does so now. And so men will, I think,
    Till the end of time.

            Cornel. Why yes; for so 't is said,
To him, who much hath, shall be given much,
And, who hath little, from him shall be reft
The little that he hath. Poor Montanino,
Being brought to the verge of ruin by the sin
Of his wrong-headed ancestors, must now
Be penn'd up in a dungeon!

            Domicil. For his own.
'T is coat and cloak most truly. But I doubt
He has deserv'd to lose them.

            Cornel. O my Aunt!
With that good heart of thine, how canst thou judge
So harshly? And such cause of family feud!
'T is but a dog and a wild boar after all!

Domicil. No, 't was a man's life taken, Massimino,
    One of the best of the Salimbeni, slain
    By Niccolò Montanino, a wild youth
    Whose heart's blood altogether was not worth
    One drop of Massimino's! That one drop
    Has bled two hundred years, and still will bleed
    While beats a heart with Montanini's pulse.

Cornel. Now Heaven forefend! But tell me, dear my aunt,
    How this fell out. I cannot keep the count
    For twice a hundred years.

            Domicil. Ah, times are chang'd!
    In my day, damsels of a noble house

Knew all their lineage, and could trace their blood
Back to Rome's consuls, were the race so long.
Cornel. It must have run a stream as long as the Arbia,[15]
And not so pure as what supplies our fountains.
Domicil. Thou art degenerate! no true Salimbene.
Cornel. Forgive me, Aunt; I needs must be amus'd,
To hear of families whose noble blood
Bubbled before the she-wolf had a lair.[16]
I thought we were of the oldest and the best.
Domicil. And so we are, as ancient and as good
As the Tolomei. · Then come Saracini,
And Piccolo'mini, and Malavolti.
The Montanini are behind all these. —
But to my tale.
                Two hundred years ago,
Soon after the great Countess[17] quit the world,
Bequeathing to the Pope what was not hers
To give away, and the Sane'si[18] freed
Had not yet driven out their bravest and best,
And us'd their footcloth for a diadem —
Cornel. That means, while yet the nobles rul'd.
                    Domicil. What else?

Upon a certain day, a numerous party
Of high-born youth rode out to hunt the boar.
On the return, discoursing of their feats,
Whose hounds were foremost, strongest, and most bold,
The Salimbeni claim'd the day as theirs,
The Montanini theirs. The strife wax'd hot.
From words it came to blows: and swords were drawn:
VOL. IV.—13

And Niccolò Montanino, mad with rage,
Smote Massimino of the Salimbeni
Dead on the field.   Thence vengeance.   Thence the feud;
Which rag'd, at intervals, twice eightscore years;
Till, stript of all their castles, and their race
Almost exhausted, (for the Salimbeni,
The richest and most widely branching house
In all Siena, greatly overmatch'd them,)
The Montanini quench'd, the fire burn'd out.
But there the cinders,are, and smoulder still.

Cornel. And who would stir them?   Not my brother, sure.
Poor Montanino! if thy sires were bloody,
Thy beggar'd fortunes and thy dwindled race
Have made atonement!

          Domicil. Why, Cornelia, child!
Thou hadst better fall in love with Messer Carlo,
And build the house up!

          Cornel. Not so far as that:
I am no mason.   But I tell thee, Aunt,
Light as I am, I have reason strong enough,
And heart I hope, to hold these feuds in horror.
And more, I dare avow, young Montanino,
Last of his race and with his ruin'd fortune,
Alone with that sweet sister, both so sad,
And both so noble in their gentle mien,
Has for my heart and fancy more attraction
Than any of my brother's happier friends.
I think how I should like to draw him near
And smile away his sadness, and to make

That dear Angelica my bosom's friend.

Domicil. Why, did I ever! —— No, when I was young,

    A maiden had as soon bit off her tongue,

    As prais'd an enemy.   And I suppose,

    Now that the youth is prison'd for some crime,

    Thou 'lt make a saint of him.

                    Cornel. That is to see.

Here Antonello comes.   I bade him learn

What had transpired.

              Domicil. Thou didst?   The girl is mad!

Why, in my day! —— Ah, times indeed are chang'd!

I wonder how the world will get along!

Enter ANTONELLO.

Cornel. Why very much as though no Montanino

    Nor Salimbene were in 't!   We are but bubbles

    Floating upon some portion of the flood,

    Which, whether we break at once or swim awhile,

    Rolls downward to the ocean, all the same. —

    Well, Antonello?

              Domicil. Really!   I did never! —

Anton. [*He speaks throughout, though still quickly, yet more de-*

        liberately, through respect, than when with Barbara.

I met with Monna Gelica's[19] young maid,

Who had told me of her master's taking up,

Madonna, as you know.

            Cornel. And what said *she?*

Anton. He has been charg'd before the Nine with practising

    With the Messeri of the Tolomei

To bring the exil'd nobles back again.

Domicil. Plotting with Deo of the Tolomei,

The banish'd Guelf! [20]   What say'st thou, child, to that?

Cornel. 'T is, Aunt, a mere political offence, —

Rebellion, — even if the charge be prov'd.

Domicil. Don't contradict me, child : I say, 't is crime.

Leag'd with the Tolomei to expel

The Salimbeni!   Said I not he was

Our house's foe !   Is 't prov'd ? [*to Anton.*

Anton. Madonna, yes.

Domicil. And what his punishment ?

Anton. Condemn'd to pay

A thousand florins,[21] or to lose his head.

Cornel. 'T is tyranny !   Ippolito so will say.

That poor Angelica! and her brother's life !

Domicil. Ippolito will say no such a thing.

And poor Angelica need not be concern'd :

Their friends will pay the fine and save his life. —

Plotting with Deo of the Tolomei,

The banish'd Guelf!   I told thee that the cinders

Were smouldering still.   But thou wouldst not believe.

Young folk were not so headstrong in my day.

[*Exit Domicil.*

Cornel. Is Messer Carlo really condemn'd ?

Anton. I stood before the Palace of the Signory.

Men talk'd of nothing else.   They say, he is given

Two weeks to pay the mulct in.

Cornel. Poor young lady !

How did she bear it ?

Anton. As you may suppose,
Knowing, Madonna, that her brother was
A god in the lady's eyes. She swoon'd away.
I wish my master were return'd!

           • *Cornel.* For what?

Anton. I don't know, Monna Nelia. But you see —
Monna Angelica is the sweetest creature!
My master is — I think —— An angel quite!

Cornel. Thy master?

        Anton. Monna Gelica, I mean.

Cornel. I think so too, good Nello. Say no more.
Learn all thou canst. And, hark thou! if it be
Thou hear'st the desolate lady is in need
Of aught that I can furnish, let me know.
I will supply it. Only, have a care
She shall not know the true source whence it comes.

Anton. God's life! Madonna, thou 'rt an angel too!

Cornel. Thou knowest, Madonna Angelica and I
Are neighbors, and good manners spread by contact.
Go now, hear all, and see all; but thy mouth,
For Salimbene's honor, keep thou close!

       [*Exit, joyfully, but with marked respect, Anton.*
I would too that Ippolito were back!
What will he do? He loves that lovely lady
Better than life. And say what will my aunt,
He has no feeling of enmity for the brother,
But thinks as I do of these silly feuds.
I would I durst inform her of his love!
But her kind heart is so o'ergrown with weeds

Of genealogy and family pride,
They choke the wheat of sense and Christian grace.
To think of fighting for a pack of hounds!
And a whole family spent for one boar's blood!
I wonder not the people are sick of rank
And shut ancestral honors from their gates.
If Carlo Montanino sought to open them,
His head is not so solid as it looks,
And might, for all its use, as well be off.

[*Turns to make her Exit, in same direction as Domicilla,*

and Scene closes.

Scene II.

A cell in the public prison.

CARLO,
*seated on a bench apparently of stone, and leaning
pensively on a small table of seemingly similar material, his
forehead on his hand.
A noise within, as of bolts withdrawn,
and a narrow vaulted door, at the right, opens.   A* JAILER
gives admittance to BECCARI, *and then, at a sign
from the latter, shuts in the two
together.*

Becc. [*after a moment — Carlo not rising.*
You sent for me, Messere.   I have come.
        CARLO, *dropping his hand, looks at him steadily,
        but does not rise.*
Will it please you speak?   'T is not a thing most usual
For a high Signor of the State to wait
On a convicted culprit.
        CARLO *rises with dignity, and comes forward with
        an air of tranquil yet melancholy majesty, and
        speaks in a tone corresponding to his mien.*
                Carlo. I am not —
Neither culprit, nor convicted ; though condemn'd,
I feel, most truly, and condemn'd unjustly.
I had no thought, Messer', to wound your pride.

You were not of the bench which took away
My liberty on a perjur'd charge, sustain'd
By no clear evidence, and against whose substance
I was not suffer'd even to protest.

Becc. I was not on the bench; but being of those
Who judg'd and who condemn'd you, must not hear
Their justice call'd in question.   Not for me
To sentence you unheard; nor will you credit,
That I, whom 't not concerns, should greatly care
Whether you be or innocent or not.
But all men are my brothers, and as man
My heart can throb with sympathy for those
Whom as a magistrate my tongue must censure.
For this, and for your noble sister's sake ——

Carlo. [*quietly, yet with slight severity.*

My sister leave alone, and speak of me.

Becc. Why hinder that an angel come between
Our earthy natures, and make smooth a path
That either may without her find too rough?

Carlo. [*with increased severity, yet without passion.*

Messer', Messere'! this is to abuse
Our several positions.   What you mean
I know not, but between yourself and me
Is no affair wherein my sister mingles.

Becc. Well, Messer Carlo Montanino, well.
I thought you had found need of me, and came
To offer help.   Why sent you for me then?

Carlo. Ser Gasparo Beccari, oftentimes
You have sued to me to have my only farm

Down in the vale of Strovè, and late offer'd
Up to twelve hundred florins, which I refus'd,
Not willing then to sell at any price.
My need now is ascendant.   Take the farm.
Becc. No, Messer Montanino ; times are chang'd.
To tempt you, I made offers far above
The actual value.   These you chose, from pride,
Or fancy, or whatever cause you will,
Flatly to set at nought.   'T is now my turn.
You ask to sell.   I will not give you now
Twelve hundred florins.
    Carlo. I had not suppos'd
You wish'd to chaffer.
    Becc. Then you quite forgot
I am a merchant, as your foresires were,
And were, 't is not yet threescore years gone by,
The great destroyers of your lesser race,
The wealthy Salimbeni; wiser they,
And better patriots, who could lend the State
For one emergence twenty thousand florins
Out of their private coffers.
    Carlo. But well secur'd.[22]
What boots this reminiscence ?   That my sires
Were not of the dominant faction, let my need,
And that I am now imprison'd on a charge
Utterly false, untried, without a word
Permitted in defence, and doom'd to lose
My life, or pay a fine beyond my means,
Let this attest, and plead for your forbearance ;
 13*

Nor seek to wound who casts no stone at you.

Becc. I might reply, Messere, that you have,
Though it fell short. But let us pass that over.
Our talk is now of money. He who bids
For what is not on sale must offer largely.
I did so. Who would sell where is no bid,
Must tempt with easy prices. You do not.
I dropp'd the magistrate at your desire;
I can resume it, so please you, and withdraw. [*turns to go.*

Carlo. Yet stay.

He walks up the stage. BECCARI *watches him with a look of
exultant malignity, which he instantly suppresses, when*
CARLO, *returning, raises his head and resumes.*

'T is hard. But I have no resource.
Give me a thousand florins, and take the farm.

Becc. 'T was my first offer, truly. But remember,
I bade you note 't was much beyond its worth.
'T is you that wish to sell, not I to buy.
The case is alter'd.

        Carlo. Do I hear aright?
Is this your charity?

        Becc. 'T is my common sense.
I wonder you not see it.

        Carlo. 'T is because
You sought to blind me with your Christian love
And human sympathy.

        Becc. That was no blind.
I hold all men my brothers, and I sorrow
For you as for all others, but no more.

I do to you what you would do to me
Under like circumstances.

> *Carlo.* [*loftily, and with more of passion
> than he has hitherto betrayed.*

Never! No,
Not were you my worst enemy.

> *Becc.* So you think.

It is but your opinion.   I have mine.
I am a stranger to your class as blood,
A man of the people : why do you appeal
To me, when you have friends of your own rank?
Your father's blood is lessen'd to the veins
Of only two : but yet your mother's flows
In a fair stream.   Not wholly are you spent,
Nor quite alone.   There are who boast your kin
Who are rich, though happily for the public peace
And common weal they are no more of note.
Why in your urgence not solicit them ?

Carlo. You ask to mock me, knowing well ere this
They had freed me, were 't their will.   They haply dread,
Being of a faction hated by your rule,
To fall into suspicion, lend they aid
To a suspected rebel.

> *Becc.* Lo you now !

Your mother's blood grows niggard, and the friends
Of your own faction pale before the terror
Of charg'd complicity, yet you call on me
A Ghibeline and an alien to your race,
A ruler in the city which condemns you,

To lend you aid, and venture my good name
With my associate rulers and the people
Whose interests by so doing I may betray!
Well, I will venture; I have come for that;
And let your conscience after bid you blush,
That you have cast a slur upon my charity
And Christian love.   Messer Carlo Montanino,
I will take your land in Strove at its worth.
The residue to make up your amercement
May easily be found : so much your friends
May lend, nor give suspicion to the State.

Carlo. What is your offer ?

     Becc. What the farm would bring
To-morrow were it set to public sale :
Seven hundred florins.

    Carlo. Let our parle here cease.
The o'erstrain'd tyranny which has sent me hither,
An innocent man, to ruin or to death,
Is not more odious than the skulking malice
Which flouts my poverty and the rampant avarice
Which drives a bargain with my mortal need,
Usurping blasphemously the pure name
Of Christian charity.   There is the door.

    [*said loftily, but with a melancholy*
     majesty that is above passion.

  While BECCARI *replies, the cell door is again*
   thrown open, and the JAILER *admits*
    ANGELICA *and* BARBARA.

BARBARA *remains in the background.* ANGELICA *without*
a word throws herself upon CARLO'S *breast, who*
presses her there in silence until BECCARI,
whom he does not from this time
regard, has made his Exit.

Becc. Since I am here invited, Messer Carlo,
 You should have left me to depart unbidden.
 Your insult on the magistral authority
 I shall not to your detriment report.
 Your obloquy of me, and most ungrateful
 Perversion of my meaning, I shall strive,
 More for that noble lady's sake than yours,
 To not remember, and for her sweet sake
 Will do you service yet despite yourself.
 Meanwhile, peace with you! — Jailer, let me forth.
     [knocks at the door, which is open'd.
      Exit Beccari.

Angel. Oh Carlo! is all hopeless? Oh my brother!
Carlo. [*raising her from his breast*
   and kissing her on the forehead.
 Why ask, Angelica? Was thy quest in vain?
 Bertuccio Arrigucci will not aid me?
Angel. Alas! he listen'd kindly, seem'd surpris'd
 To hear of thy embarrassment, and distress'd
 To think he must refuse; because, he said,
 His known attachment to the banish'd side,
 And his affinity, through his son Rugiero,
 With Messer Sozzo Dei, made it for him

More dangerous than for others to lend thee aid.
He wonder'd that you did not sell your farm,
Which must he thought bring full a thousand florins.

Carlo. Thus all of them prepare to see me die!
I was unjust to accuse this butcher's son,
The associate of a tyrannous popular rule,
Of want of charity and malicious will,
When my own kindred and best-trusted friends,
To escape suspicion and a possible fine,
Selfishly give me over to the axe.
What though they should affront even risk of exile,
Or sequestration of all worldly goods,
Is not my blood in the scale? And were theirs balanc'd,
Would not I venture more? even life as well?
But no! that is for me to exact too much.
Nor do I do it, Angelica. Yet — and yet —
Why did not my rich cousin advance the means
To others less obnoxious, and through *them*
Have got me clear?

        Angel. 'T is like he did not think it.
I will to him instantly and urge the plan.

Carlo. No; he will tell thee that the State would trace
The ransom to its source and make him answer.
Thou shalt not blush, nor for thyself nor me,
At his renew'd refusal.

        Angel. In such a case
There can be nought to blush for. Rather shame
Is his who, in an hour of mortal need,
Denies a kinsman aid, than his who asks it.

Oh let me back, my brother! if not to him,
Yet to some other.   Do not shake thy head!
Where life is hope is, and it cannot be
All will repel us.

      Carlo. I do fear it will.
There is none to us allied, remote or near,
That is not fallen into some suspect
With the malignant Nine, or will not plead
Their jealous fears, to avoid the doing of what
Might haply move suspicion.   No, believe me,
He who would aid me will not need be ask'd.

Angel. Then must we sell our pretty place in Strovè.
Do it, dear Carlo, and quit this fearful den.

Carlo. Poor child! . And wilt thou tell me how to sell?
Didst thou not mark Beccari's mood in parting?

Angel. Something I noted in his tone: not much.
He seem'd to have been repuls'd.   He came to buy?

Carlo. Doubtful, since others fail'd me, that Bertuccio
Would listen even to thee, I sent to speak
With Ser Beccari, and had from him a lesson
Was hardly needed.

      Angel. What was that, my brother?

Carlo. Thou hast mark'd, among the gentlest even of birds,
How when one sickens, or is broken-wing'd,
The rest will peck at him, nay oftentimes
The male at the wounded female.   So with men.
The strong, who need no help, have help in plenty.
'T is press'd upon them even against their will.
The feeble cry in vain; their happier brothers

Pluck at their feathers and worry them to death.

Angel. No, Carlo, not with all. [*embracing him.*

    Carlo. No, Earth were Hell,
Were there no angels in it.   But thou, my cherub,
Thy wing is broken too.

    Angel. Thou dost not mean,
We cling together only that we both
Are poor and helpless?

    Carlo. No; thought I that,
The headsman's axe were welcome.   Said I not,
Thou art an angel?   While thou tread'st its walks
Earth still has Paradise, and therefore only,
For thy sweet sake, I struggle yet to live. —
But to the means of life — which yet I see not.
Beccari offer'd for the farm, thou knowest,
Twelve hundred florins.   Then, I could refuse.
Now I must offer, he will not give me more
Than seven hundred.   'T is the law of trade.
So he would teach me.   But I rather think it
The law of common nature.   I am down:
Why lift me up?   My body stops the way.
Let the proud trample on it, or step over,
Nor stop to ask if yet its heart beats warm.

Angel. O do not talk so desperately, dear brother!
See! through thy prison-bars the setting sun
Darts even now a line of level gold.
It has been hidden all the livelong day.
Accept the omen, Carlo: trust in God,
Who will not leave thy virtue unrepaid.

Carlo. No, thine, sweet saint: mine has no note in Heaven:
This ray of sunset fortune shines for thee.
Be it! I shall die happy.
                    Angel. Carlo! Carlo!
This doubt tempts Providence: and this despair,
Is it for me to listen?
                    Carlo. No, forgive me.
I will for thy sake think what may be done.
Angel. Think not, but act! Command the farm be sold!
Bertuccio valued it a thousand florins.
Carlo. Well, I will ponder. Sleep thou undisturb'd.
                                        [*stooping to kiss her.*
Angel. [*throwing herself on his neck.*
Sleep undisturb'd! while thou art pillow'd here?
Carlo. Fi, fi! is this thy trust in Heaven? See now!
Thou art making good Barbara herself to cry!
Cheer up, my sister! — So! — Knock, Barba, now.
                    [*Barb. knocks on the portal, which is
                        opened by the Jailer.*
Good even, Angelica. [*embracing her.*
                    Angel. Do sell the farm!
Do, do, my brother! [*kisses him fondly and repeatedly,
                    then, going out, suddenly comes back, and
                        embraces him silently, and Exit,
                            followed by Barbara.
                    The door is closed, and the
                    bolts are heard within.*
                    Carlo. And what wouldst thou then do?
Must I give thee to beggary? thee? I will

Indeed well ponder it. — The ray is fied.

> [*looking off the scene.*

It came with thee, and would not stay, thou gone.
And now, without that double light, these walls
Are blacker than before. — O guard her, Heaven!
With me do even as befits Thy Will,
But have, I pray, have mercy upon her!

He walks up the stage, and Scene closes.

Scene III.

*The Entrance of the Palazzo Montanini within.
The Background presents the Great Gate
closed. On the Right, the lower
steps of a winding staircase.
On the Left, the Por-
ter's Lodge.
Knocking without.*

Enter GIANNI from the Lodge.

Gianni. Now, who can that be, knocking at the gate?
You 'll not get in, I 'm thinking! now! — St. John!

You 're in a hurry!

Moving slowly to the gate.] But there takes one more
 To give you speed; and that 's not I.   I 'll see,
 However, who you be: it is n't safe,
 Now everybody 's out —— Ay, ay, I hear!
  [*draws a slide covering a latticed loophole and looks out.*
 Hum! Ser Beccari!   What wants he, I wonder.
  [*Opens partially a postern in the great door and,*
    looking out,
 The mistress 's out; and Barbara is out;
 The master 's where nobody better knows
 Than you, I 'm thinking.   So you can't come in,
 Messer Beccari. [*offering to shut the postern.*
    It is pushed back, and, brushing by him,

          Enter BECCARI.

          Becc. Never mind, my friend,
 I 'll wait thy mistress.
          Gian. Mistress is n't us'd
 To be awaited.   She is where she ought,
 Consoling my poor master, Messer Carlo,
 Who 's where he ought not; greater shame to those
 Who put him there! and won't be home till dark.
Becc. That won't be long; the sun is setting now.
 Come, my good Gianni; thou 'rt a brave old fellow,
 Plain, downright, honest stuff, such as I like;
 And ——
Gian. No, I a'n't; nor plain, nor honest more

Than other folk, I 'm thinking; but I know
Just what I like and what I don't like, and
I show it.

   Becc. And that 's downright.

       Gian. No, it is n't;
It 's natural: that 's my idea.

      Becc. Well, be it.
It is thy nature, Gianni, and 't is mine,
To show our likings. And I do so now.
Come, there is money. [*Gianni looks at it wistfully, but*
       turns away.

     Nay, my frank old man;
'T is frankly offer'd; and I know thou need'st it;
Ye are not over well provided here.

Gian. I say we are: who told you we were not?
.And I can take no pay but from the master.
Put up your money: you are tempting me
To nothing good, I 'm thinking; but you won't
Succeed: that 's my idea.

     Becc. If I had thought to,
I had not try'd to tempt thee, as thou call'st it.
No, good old man, I am thy master's friend,
Although he does not know it; would gladly aid him,
As I would all the unhappy of mankind.

Gian. [*who has shook his head distrustfully while*
  Becc. spoke.
  But I am not unhappy.

     Becc. Peace! — It is
Because I know thee loyal to thy lord

I seek to do thee kindness.   Take it! [*offering again the*
money.   Gianni looks wistfully and sidelong at it, as be-
fore, but struggles with his desire, and shakes his head.

No?

Well then, some other time.   And 't is for this,
My wish to serve thy master spite himself,
I 'd speak with thy young mistress.   Tell me now —
Thou knowest, good Gianni — of what mood is she?
Gian. Eh?

  Becc. Of what temper, disposition?

Gian. Oh!

The same as Master's.

Becc. So?   I should have thought

They hardly were alike.   And what is his?
Gian. The same as mine : he don't like strangers.   So,
  Please to go out, Messer Beccari.

Becc. Come!

Please to remember what I am.

Gian. I do.

You are one of our rulers, the more shame for you.
The people do not like you any more
Than do the nobles; only, these dare not
Speak out their minds, as dare the people, and I,
Because you cannot hurt me, since I am
Not worth the hurting.   But you are a set
Of shabby tyrants, and you know it; and
The sooner we are rid of you, the better.[29]
That 's my idea.

Becc. Plain, downright, honest Gianni!

Dost recollect, though I may not hurt *thee*,
These sentiments, reported as thy master's,
May hurt him?

      Gian. Well; he is in prison, is n't he?
And I don't know but that you put him there.
Becc. I? No! I should be glad to get him out.
Gian. Well, do it then: that 's better than to say it:
And I shall think the better of you. But
You cannot do it here: and, as Madonna
Is not at home, I wish you would go out.
That 's my idea.

      Becc. [*turning to go.*
      It 's my idea, my friend,   .
Thou dost not know thy right foot from thy left.
But I shall come to-morrow; and thou 'lt see
I am thy lady's right hand in this strait.
Commend me to her, and tell her I so said.

Gian. [*opening the postern.*
    I 'll tell her that a magistrate was here,
And recommend her not to have to do
With any of that sort. That 's my idea.

                  [*Exit Beccari.*.

Good even, Ser Beccari. —
    Shutting the door.] And the Devil
Go with you, and the like of you! — I 'm glad
He 's gone. Madonna will come home
Quite sad enough from poor dear Master's prison,
Without this beast to make her cry, I 'm thinking.
He 's got long claws, I 'll warrant, though he purs.

I 've seen the kind before ; you rub the fur
A little rough, and out the nails come sharp. --
'T is time she was a-coming. I 'll look out.

          [opening again the postern.

O Messer Carlo, it will break her heart
It they should kill you ! and I think 't will mine.

    He puts his head out at the opening, and

        Scene closes.

ACT THE THIRD

SCENE I.   *As in Act I. Scene I.*

ANGELICA

coming slowly forward to BECCARI, *who, bowing profoundly,*
appears to have just entered ; BARBARA *also ad-*
vancing, but keeping behind her mistress,
a little in the background.

Becc. Madonna, does this moment find you free ?
Angel. As free as at a time of such distress
    I can be.   What is Ser Beccari's pleasure ?
Becc. To do away, Madonna, that distress,
    If so it please you.   In your own hand lies
    Your brother's destiny.
                        Angel. In mine?   In mine?
    And I not know it ?   But you are of the Nine.
    Speak, speak, Messer'!   Why has he languish'd then
    Ten days in prison ?   I do not understand you.
    In my hand ?   Speak!
                        Becc. In thine, most truly, lady.
    Had I obey'd my feelings, I had come
    Five days ago to see you, as I promis'd
    That evening when you loiter'd at the prison
    And your rude porter would not let me wait.

Angel. O do not call him rude, that good old man!
  He is but loyal; 't is our house's sorrow
  Has fill'd him with distrust.

                    Becc. I do not blame him;
  He follows but the master's gloomy lead.
  And 't is for this alone his captious humor
  Deserves my mention.   Pride and cold disdain
  . Meet, on your brother's part, my Christian offers,
  And my best efforts are thwarted by distrust.

Angel. [*losing her animation, and resuming the air of dignity and
     reserve with which she had met Beccari.*
  You do remind me.   'T is that you yourself
  Have given him cause to judge you harshly.

                    Becc. How?
  I came to him to offer for his farm;
  And did so largely.   He refus'd, and haughtily.

Angel. I think not: haughtiness is not his vice.

Becc. No, 't is his weakness.

                    [*Angel. evinces pain and displeasure.*
                    Pardon!   I meant not
  To ruffle feelings which I most revere.
  He did refuse: Madonna, you were by.

Angel. He wish'd not then to sell.   But, chang'd the case,
  He sent for you; and then you did reject
  The terms you had offer'd.

                    Becc. 'T was, the case was chang'd.

Angel. What! do you drive a traffic with distress,
  And in the emergence of a mortal need
  Find pretext to enhance the means of aid?

Becc. Why not, young lady? Do not all men so?
 I ask'd your brother, and I ask you now,
 Why do not his own friends, your mother's kin,
 Assist him?
   Angel. Wo is us! they dare not do it.
 But you, Messere, dare.
     Becc. No more than they.
 Might I not be suspected too? 'No, lady,
 Your brother, Messer Carlo, has not had
 That deference for me he should have had.
 I would befriend him. Will you let me so?
 Look at the Salimbeni, his destroyers ——
Angel. Wrong not the innocent!
     Becc. Pardon! I should say,
 Destroyers of his race. What gave them power?
 They owe it not to their enormous wealth,[24]
 But to their influence with the popular party,
 Their union with the dominant cause, through which
 They drove their sole great rivals from the State.
Angel. To what tends this? I own, Messer Beccari,
 You are of the Nine; and therefore more I wonder,
 That having the power, and the will professing,
 To aid my hapless brother in this strait,
 You but parade it, and not use it.
     Becc. Lady,
 I only bid you mark it, in the hope
 You now will bid me use it; for on you,
 And you alone, depends it that I do.
Angel. What mean you?

Becc. Said I not, that in your hands
Lies your lov'd brother's destiny ?

    Angel. Explain.

Keep me not anxious !

    Becc. Bid your servant then,
I pray you of your courtesy, for my sake,
Withdraw a brief while.

    Angel. Backward a few steps,
Out of all hearing, if that will suffice.

Becc. If so it must be.

    Angel. Barbara, retire ;
But keep in sight.

  BARBARA *goes up the stage, but very soon, when*
  BECCARI *has ceased to observe her, moves*
   nearer by degrees, and listens.

    Now briefly.

    Becc. [*looking back, then in a*
     lower tone.

    Were, Madonna,
Your brother my ally ; in other words,
Our interests made one ——

    Angel. That cannot be.
Not for his life would Carlo change his faction,
Were not his sentiments first chang'd.

    Becc. Dear lady,
You do misapprehend me.   Not through him
The alliance I propose, but — dare I say 't ?

Through you.

   Angel. Speak more conceivably, Messere.

Becc. I see around in these disfurnish'd rooms
No mirror hung, or I would bid you look,
And there receive my answer.

     Angel. Barbara!

       Becc. Nay,
Call her not to you.   Think! in five days more,
Your brother's life is forfeit.   Will you not
Reach out a hand to save him?

     Angel. By what means?

Becc. By lifting up the fortune I would lay
At your fair feet, and with it lifting me.

Angel. Never!   I trust in Heaven; nor will I stoop
To even listen to what is shame from one
Who builds his hopes of winning me — since so
I needs must understand you — on the ruin
Of my own brother.   Come, Barbara.

     Becc. Lady, no!
By your own gentle self, I pray! one word!
Think not so meanly of me, deem me not
So senseless-daring, had I even the heart,
To offer in exchange your brother's life
For the high honor of your hand.   Believing
I am too humble, having in myself
No claim to do you homage ——

     Angel. Cease, Messere.
In any way I would not listen; but this
I may advise: — to win the right to plead,

You should have set my innocent brother free,
Then come to me.

             Becc. And would you then have listen'd?
May I then hope, dear lady, if I give
Your brother to your arms again? ——

                   Angel. Hope nothing,
Messer Beccari, that is not in truth
And reason. If indeed you use the power
You seem now to avow, nay, if you keep
Simply your proffer'd terms, and for the farm
Pay down my brother's ransom, then, sir, then,
Come to his sister, and you shall receive
All that a truly grateful heart can pay,
My first of benefactors and my friend.

Becc. And nothing more but this?

                 Angel. And nothing more:
Since nothing more can be. What would you more?
O Ser Beccari! give again to life
My father's son, and thou shalt be to me
A second father!

             Becc. You mistake, Madonna;
I am but one of Nine, and have no power
To free your brother, though Heaven knows my wish
Leans heartily that way. To purge him clear
Of the strong charge of treason to the State,
Nay more, to give him influence in the State,
Build up his ruin'd fortunes, and his head,
Which the axe threatens, lift as high as the best
Of the Salimbeni, this was in my will.

But the sole means to compass it you would not,
Scorning my honest love. —

   Angel. I have said, Messere!
In any way I will not listen that.
Cease then to urge it. Not to build his fortune
Thought I to accept your proffer'd aid, for *that*
My brother would disdain from any man.
He has offer'd you, upon your own urg'd terms,
The estate in Strove. Was it ten days since
A thousand florins worth, 't is not less now.
Bertuccio Arragucci counts it that.
Take it, and for the urgence of our need
Become our benefactor. Said I more?
Thou shalt be, truly shalt thou be, my friend,
My second father.

   Becc. If the Ser Bertuccio,
Your mother's cousin, lends not, why should I,
My risk is greater, brave the State's suspect?
Lady, I am a merchant; I can give
Nothing for nothing; and my profits vary
According to the need which makes my ware
Rise in the mart or fall. I would not be
Your second father; I would rather be,
That which your beauty and excelling virtue
Make foremost of my wishes, your first spouse.
Hear me then. —

   Angel. Barbara, come. The Ser Beccari
Can as before alone find out his way.

      [*Exeunt Angel. and Barb.*

Becc. Distraction! 'T is the same accursed pride
  Deep-set in both, though putting forth diversely,
  According to the soil wherein 't is grown.
  I 'll pluck it up by the roots, or I will die for 't!

                              [*turning to go.*

                    Enter GIANNI.

Gian. Well, you have seen at last Madonna Gelica.
  I hope you are satisfied, Messer' Beccari?
  You 've found she don't like magistrates, I 'm thinking.
  You 'd best not come again, that 's my idea.
  And so, I 'll show you out, if so you 're done.
Becc. Silence, old fool! And lead the way. I am done
  For the present — *here.*   .
            Gian. Come. [*leading off.*] Better an old fool,
  Than be a sinner at any age, I 'm thinking.
      [*Stops at the Exit, to give the advance to Becc.*

                              Exit Becc.
  And so you 'll find one day — that 's my idea.

                              [*Exit Gianni.*

SCENE II.

As in Act II. Scene I.

IPPOLITO. CORNELIA. DOMICILLA.

Ippol. Now, Aunt Docilla, now, Cornelia dear,
    Ippolito has told you all his fortunes
    By stream and horsepath, forest, dell, and hill,
    Since his prodigious absence of ten days, —
    And, 'sooth, it has seem'd wondrous long indeed,
    Parted from your dear loves! —
                    Cornel. O fi, Ippol'to!
    Parted from *our* dear loves?   And is that *all*
                    [*looking at him archly.*
    That weigh'd upon the sluggish wing of Time?
Domicil. And what beside should load the hours for him?
    Thou dost injustice to thy brother's love.
Cornel. No, I do perfect justice to his love.
    Don't I, Ippolito? [*same manner.*
            Domicil. Child, don't contradict.
    Thou interrupt'st him.   Do as thou seest me.
    When I was young, a damsel would have blush'd
    To cut the thread short of her brother's tale.
    But times are chang'd.
            Cornel. 'T is well they are, dear Aunt,

Since it may do a pleasure to one's brother
To cut his thread off or make short his tale.
I am sure I have done so now.

     Domicil. Go on, my son.
Don't mind her: in her joy to have thee back,
She talks a deal of nonsense.

     Ippol. Let her, Aunt!
I like it well: it helps digestion.   Then,
My thread was well nigh spent.   I meant to say,
Now I have made you merry with my journey
And scenes abroad, lift you the curtain here,
And show what 's new since I left Vito's gate.
Say thou, Cornelia.

     Cornel. Hast thou not then heard?
Ippol. Nothing that 's strange.   Siena is, I take it,
Not any sager being ten days older,
But the same seething pot of faction still.
The Devil can find none hotter, save what boils
On our near neighbors' fires; Arezzo, Pisa,
Florence, all help to keep each other little;
And so Italia's states will do, I suppose,
To the end of time, with foreign greater powers
To egg them on, who find in their dissensions
The means to keep them separate and thus weak.
But Aunt, I see, don't think *me* ten days wiser,
Who 've come back harping on the same old string.
Come, what 's to tell, Cornelia?   Is it jocund?
Cornel. So Aunt thinks: but I say, 't will make thee sad.
Domicil. I say, 't will not.   Though, times are greatly chang'd
 14*

Since I was young.

        Ippol. Not quite: tastes differ still.

But let us hear.

        Cornel. Poor Carlo Montanino ——

Ippol. Not dead ?

        Cornel. No, but condemn'd to die, within

Five days, unless ——

        Ippol. Good Heaven! what has he done ?

Domicil. What might be thought of him: conspir'd, my child,

Against the State.

        Ippol. Conspir'd against the State ?

What might be thought of him ? . Why, Aunt Docilla,

Almost as soon I had thought it of myself!

Cornel. There, Aunt!

        Ippol. Why surely, you would not rejoice

To have him dead ?

        Domicil. Giesu forbid! But dead

He is not like to be :. a thousand florins,

Cost what they will, may sometime be replac'd ;

Never a head.

        Ippol. A thousand florins ? [*in perplexity.*

        Cornel. Aunt

Is not quite right. The poor young man stands charg'd

With leaguing to bring back the banish'd nobles.

Domicil. And is n't that the same ? Child, thou art rude !

Ippol. Not quite the same. I could not think him guilty

Of plotting against his country ; but conspiring

To unseat the powers that be is lighter guilt,

And not unlikely.

Domicil. How thou talk'st, Ippol'to!
Why, it is Carlo Montanino plotting
The restoration of our deadliest foe,
The puissant Tolomei! Hear'st thou that?

Ippol. Puissant enough: but *he* is weak, and humbled,
Forget it not! through us. A thousand florins
Will ruin him.

      Domicil. Is 't my brother's son that speaks?
The blood of Massimino Salimbene ——

Ippol. Shed now two hundred years is all too dry
To fructify mischief, if there lie one seed
Of such in my breast for Carlo Montanino.

Domicil. And thou canst pity him! Times indeed are chang'd!

Ippol. The last male scion of an ancient house
Reduc'd to poverty by his foresire's fault!
I would my foresires had no hand in it!
He is a fine young fellow: I wish him well.

Domicil. Thy father had not thought this. In my day ——

Ippol. In thy day, Aunt, my father's self had shudder'd
To tread upon a corpse. Was 't not an ass
That kick'd at the dead lion? Wouldst thou have *me*
Even such a brute? thy pet Ippolito
Whom thy dear lips have flatter'd into pride?

Domicil. No, no, my child! my boy! But yet ——

                Ippol. But yet,
Even if this be prov'd ——

      Cornel. It is not prov'd!
They would not let him answer in defence!
They hurried him to prison on the instant,

Doom'd to pay down the fine, or lose his head.

Ippol. The devil! Why this is tyranny unmask'd!

Be this the way the Nine abuse the laws,

I 'll join, myself, to drive the monsters out.

Domicil. Hush, hush! don't say it! thou 'rt mad!

                                Ippol. By Heaven, Aunt,

I believe we all in Italy are mad!

People against nobles, nobles 'gainst the people,

Cities all striving to cut each other's throat,

That foreign realms may rule us: all stark mad!

And have been ever since the Roman fall.

Is it so long since Dante Alighieri,

A man, beyond all computation, worth

Ten thousand Bondelmonti and Uberti,

And whose great voice shall thunder through all time,

Stirring the pulse of millions yet to be,

In climes where not a syllable shall sound

Of Salimbene's name, dead on the page

Of histories scarcely read, — unless some bard

Should rake our ashes for a playhouse-theme

And make them live an hour, — is 't many weeks

Since Dante, by a faction driven abroad,

Died mournfully in exile? Where 's to end

This tyranny of party? this upstirring

Of blood by brother's blood? I 'm sick of it all.

Thou look'st astonish'd, Aunt; but in thy ear

I only tell thee what is hourly thought

By some of our best men, and when the Nine

Begin to totter, as they must ere long,

Some ev'n of our own name will join the hunt,
Not Piccolomini and Malavolti only,
And, with the Tolomei, chase these wolves
Out of Siena.[25]

    Domicil. And with the Tolomei?
I never thought to see this day!

                    Ippol. Why not?
Interest makes stranger matches; and we have seen
The White and Black change colors in Firenze.
This tyrant body, detested by the people
Whose guardians they profess to be, shall they
Be lov'd by us of the better class, whose rights
They have dash'd to shivers? What they now have done
To Carlo Montanino they might do
To me some day, were I as poor as he.
Fancy me, Aunt, as desolate as he,
Then wrong'd as he. Thou wouldst not praise the act?

Domicil. O no, it was base! I do not love the Nine:
They were not made in my day. But, my boy,
Speak not so boldly! These vile, upstart men,
Have now the power. For my sake ——

                    Ippol. Well, I won't.
But do have charity for poor Montanino!
And his sweet sister —— [*checks himself, while Cornelia,
                    stepping behind her aunt, makes
                    him a signal of caution.*

            Domicil. Well, my love, I see,
Thou and Cornelia still will contradict me,
And so I 'll leave you for some dumb affairs .

That claim my overlooking. [*looking off the scene.*
          Coming, Lisa. —
I 'll give thee such a meal! [*going.*
        Ippol. [*detaining her.* .
          But season it, do,
With charity for Carlo, and Angel' —[*checking himself.*
And his young sister!
      Domicil. Ah! in my young day ——
Ippol. In thy young day, young fellows lov'd their aunts
  As well as they do now.   At least, I 'm sure,
  If they were such as thou art, Aunt Docilla,
  They must have lov'd them spite of all their whims
  Of olden days. [*hugging her.*
     Domicil. Ippol'to! Ippoltino!
           [*patting him on the cheek.*
Thou mak'st a fool of me.   But in my day,
When I was young, why surely then the times
Were not the olden days.   Well, well, I hope,
The Montanino will deserve thy pity.
I 'm sure I wish the young man no great harm.
               [*Exit.*
Cornel. Thou hast mollified her hugely, artful brother!
  But had she got an inkling of thy love!
Ippol. I had not car'd.   She must ere long.
       Cornel. Have patience.
Ippol. Now tell me of Angelica.   How is she?
  What does, where is, how looks she?   Speak, Cornelia!
Cornel. Were it a time to trifle, I would tease thee
  By the hour on those questions: that I would!

I have seen her only twice.   'T was at the Duomo,
At mass.   Angelica look'd anxious, pale,
But beautiful as usual, quite an angel;
As thou and some more fools pretend to think her
Only because her name imports as much.

Ippol. Oh yes!   But thou 'rt an angel too, Cornelia,
Without the name. [*embracing her.*

   Cornel. No, I 'm the Roman matron :
My jewel is my brother.   Keep away!

       [*as he again hugs her.*

Ippol. Well said.   One day the gem shall be reset.

Cornel. Methought she look'd more lovely for her sorrow;
So touching-sad, it almost made me weep.

Ippol. Thou darling girl! [*embracing and kissing her repeatedly.*

   Cornel. Nay, art thou getting mad ?
Was Aunt then right, and wilt thou make thee gay
Over thy enemy's ruin ?   So, one's misfortune
Makes others' happiness.

   Ippol. No, rather, sister,
'T is sunshine looking brighter for the clouds.

Cornel. She goes to the prison daily, sometimes twice :
The Signory puts no restraint on that.
Now thou must know our Nello has a fancy
For Monna Angela's maid. —

   Ippol. Aha, my general!
And so ——

 Cornel. I learn what happens in poor Carlo's cell.

Ippol. Is it for Carlo's sake ?   Don't blush, Cornelia!

Cornel. I have no cause.   It is for thine, believe me,

And pity only.

　　　　Ippol. Yes, I do believe thee.
But pity is a dangerous feeling too
For a fine fellow in a woman's heart,
A heart at least like thine; and oft we end
By loving what has cost us pains to cherish.
Take care!

　　　　Cornel. Nay, never fear: I will not throw
My heart away, believe, without knowing where:
One mad one in the family 's quite enough.
Now Barbara and Nello do much better:
They talk together, and quarrel I suppose.

Ippol. Ay! 't is well turn'd: but have a care, for all:
When least we think to slip, then most we fall.

Cornel. 'T is a fair rhyme.   Thou hast had experience too.

Ippol. 'T is rhyme with reason then; and that will do.
But oh, my light heart! jesting at this time!
What of the prison?   What keeps Carlo there?

Cornel. His friends refuse to aid him, in the dread
Of being implicated.

　　　　Ippol. Coward souls!
How bitter-sharp the pang of such a wound!

Cornel. One of our precious Signors, Ser Beccari.
Had offer'd for his pretty farm in Strove
A thousand florins.   Now he will not give
But seven hundred.

　　　　Ippol. Oh, the base-born cur!
One of his father's dogs had had more heart!
What will the doom'd man do?

Cornel. He still defers,

Though daily by his sister urg'd to sell.

Ippol. And, so deferring, must embrace at last

That hound Beccari's insolent offer, and beg

A loan of the rest, perhaps too late !

                    Cornel. My brother,

I hope I have not done wrong.   Through Antonello,

I caus'd her maid to lay upon her table

A hundred florins. —

             Ippol. Ah ! [*taking her hand.*

                 And she received them,

Knowing from whom ?

            Cornel. No, Barbara was true,

I know from the result.   Her lady thinks

Bertuccio Arrigucci sent the gold.

Ippol. Bertuccio Arrigucci would not give

A single florin to save a score of lives !

And never gave in the dark. —   Go on.

                Cornel. I had

Two hundred left of my allowance, and thinking

I but forestall'd thy wishes, yester eve,

Ere the poor lady with her lonely maid

Was come from their sad visit, closely veil'd

I sought old Gianni, Montanino's porter. —

Ippol. Darling ! [*pressing the hand he still holds.*

       But why thyself?

               Cornel. I could not trust

Any but Nello ; and he had been known.

Angelica had forbidden, under pain

Of sure dismissal, her woman to receive
Anything further from an unknown source.

Ippol. Right! And old Gianni? ——

     Cornel. Hardly was persuaded,
And put queer questions, scanning me all over
As if he would remember me, and wanted
To set his cross to some receipt.   But finally
His love for the house prevail'd, and shaking long
His stubborn head, he took the "partial aid
From unknown friends."   Now brother, Carlo having
Beccari's offer, his ransom is complete.

Ippol. [*embracing tenderly his sister.*

  How I do love thee!

     Cornel. Is 't but now found out?
Love me, Ippol'to, only half so well
As Carlo is said to love his beauteous sister,
I am the first of women.

     Ippol. I can but half,
For half of my love already is that sister's.

Cornel. But half?   That's much for a lover! —   Come away:
Aunt looks for us.

     Ippol. And time it is, I was rid
Of all this dust. —   I am happy and sad at once.
My poor Angelica!   But, ah dear Cornelia!

 His arm about her tenderly, they go up the stage,

    and Scene closes.

SCENE III.

The Place of the Fountain, as in Act I. Sc. III.

BECCARI *and* GIACOMO.

Giac. Ay, but I say thou hast! cajol'd me vilely.
I am no butcher: [*Beccari scowls at him.*
     for a thousand florins
I had not perill'd young Montanino's life.
Thou mad'st me think it was to get the farm.
Becc. And so it was. Why don't he sell it then?
I bid him fairly.
   Giac. Seven hundred florins!
It is to ruin him.
  Becc. [*coldly.*] That is not my fault.
Giac. Hast thou no bowels?
     Becc. I have had for thee.
Giac. No, by St. John! but for thy niggard self
Thou shalt not let the Montanino die.
I will report thee.
   Becc. Wilt thou? And thyself?
Come, come, be less a fool. If for Camilla
Thou hast no care, have some for thy own sake.
Report me! ME! And if thy likely tale

Be credited, where wilt thou be ?   Besides,
I call upon thee then for reimbursement.
Five hundred golden florins: mark thou that !
And on the nail! five hundred golden Johns !²⁶
Now go, report me. [*Exit.*

        Giac. Cursed, cursed vice !
To make me thus a villain's senseless tool !
Me, gentle born, an unresisting slave !
The blood of innocence is on my soul ;
And yet I dare not wipe it off.   Dare not ?
Let me but see. [*pondering.*

        Some other means —— O devil !
Devil of gaming.   From the hell whereto
Thou hast brought me, let me once but struggle out,
Once breathe again the fresher wholesome air
Of really human life ! ——

*He has taken his hat off, in the heat and agitation of
the moment, to wipe his brow, — at the words, " Devil of
gaming," striking passionately his forehead with his clenched
fist, — and now thrusts out his arm at its full
length, the fist still folded, while
he walks rapidly to the
right, when*

Enter from the right, with her pitcher,
BARBARA.
She sees the movement.

    Barb. Lord ! what 's the matter ?
Why, Messer Giacomo, thou 'rt rather worse

Than Messer Gasparo was, an hour ago,
Before my lady.

> *Giac.* [*starting.*

    Hah! What 's that of Gasparo?
Speak'st thou of Gasparo Beccari, dear?

> [*chucking her under the chin.*

Barb. Come, you are all alike, you naughty men!
That 's Messer Gasparo's way : he 's making love
To everybody too, to me at once
And to my lady!

> *Giac.* And to thy lady too?

But that's no wonder. Since he has a taste
For such a tempting bit of flesh as thou, —
And, 'faith, thou 'rt devilish pretty — [*kissing her.*

> *Barb.* Go away!

Giac. And plump as a quail — [*hugging her. She affects to be
angry, and beats him off.*

    I say, I do not wonder
He has an eye for thy mistress; ye are two
Such buds of beauty. [*again kissing her.*

> *Barb.* [*coquetting, to conceal her satisfaction*

    Come now, that 's too good!
Me and my mistress! Why we 're no more like
Than pinks and sunflowers!

> *Giac.* Did I say, alike?

Now that 's the very thing; since, devil take me,
I 'd rather smell to a dainty pink like thee, [*attempting to
kiss her again. She coyly repels him.*
Than gaze at any sunflower like thy lady.

Though, tastes will differ!　Yet, I can't believe
Beccari ever did; thou 'rt such a puss!

Barb. Am I indeed!　And don't you then believe!
Well, I can tell you, he offer'd her his fortune,
And talk'd of passion like any other man.
What though he 's of the Signory, is he not
A man of bones and blood?　He try'd it hard,
And offer'd to redeem my master's life ——

Giac. Why dost thou stop?

　　　　　　　Barb. Because I talk too fast.
I had no right to tell you this.

　　　　　　　　　　Giac. No right?
A pretty girl like thee may tell a lover
Just what she likes: it 's all between the two.

Barb. Yes, but you 're not my lover, Messer Giac'mo.

Giac. A'n't I!　I have been any time six months.
I 'll prove it, an' thou 'lt let me. [*arm about her.*

　　　　　　　　　Barb. Get away!
You 're a Messere; and you make such love
As I don't want.　Besides, I don't love you.

Giac. Bah, now, that 's cruel!— Did Gasparo Beccari
Offer to save thy master, for the hand
Of Monna Angelica?　I don't believe it!　Thou hast
Mishcard; this pretty ear 's too small. [*toying with it.*

Barb. Let it alone!　it serves me well enough.
Didn't I hear him offer at her feet
To lay his fortune, if she would lift it up,
And him with it?

　　　　　　Giac. That was pretty.　And what said she?

Barb. Said? We are Montanini. [*affecting grandeur.*

　　　　　　　　　Take up, she,

A butcher's son, although he be a Signor!

She walk'd away — we both of us walk'd away,

And bade him find the door out for himself..

There now. But — [*looking off, to the left.*

　　　　　　　go away, you devil! — go! —

I must for my water. [*Goes up to the fountain.*

GIACOMO *turns off at the right, exclaiming exultingly, but*
in a smother'd voice, and with clenched hand,

　　　　　　Giac. Aha! I have thee now!

　　　　　　　　　[*Exit Giac., — while*

Enter, *simultaneously, from the left,*

ANTONELLO.

Anton. [*jerking Barb. by the elbow, while she affects to be busy*
　　　dipping.

Was n't that Messer Gradenata, with thee?

Barb. [*without turning.*

No, saucy! Say it was, what 's that to thee?

Anton. Much, if thou please; as little, an' thou like.

Barb. [*raising her pitcher to her head. He does not offer to*
　　　help her.

I suppose I may speak to just what folk I choose.

Anton. All 's one to Antonello! [*walking off whistling.*

　　　　　　　　Only then

Thou sha'n't choose me.   I should n't like my wife
To pick up such wild gentlemen, that 's all.

Barb. [who has come forward —

setting down the pitcher and crying.

O dear! O dear!   And never offer'd either
To lift for me my *brocca.*

Anton. [who has come back.] — Did n't know
Thou need'st it — put it on thyself, and down,
As if 't was easy.   Barba!   Come, don't cry:
Folks 'll be wondering.   Kiss, and let 's forgive.

Barb. I do not want to kiss and to forgive.
There 's plenty of men to kiss without forgiving.
Let me go, Nello: Monna Gelica 's gone
Alone to the prison: I must go after her:
'T is time I went.   ·

Anton. A kiss won't take much time.

Barb. I 've had enough of kissing.

Anton. Hast thou so?
Your humble servant, Donna Gradenata!
Monna Cornelia gets no news to-day. [*Exit.*

Barb. [looks after him a moment in surprise, drying her tears.
Then calling.

Nello! — Anto! — No, I won't, won't call him!
He ought to know I love him, and don't love
That saucy gentleman.   But I 'll plague his heart out!
It 's a pretty thing a body can't have eyes
And use them handsomely, without being huff'd!
Won't he come back? [*looking anxiously to the left.*

O dear! O dear! I 'll go

Straight home and cry them out. I— No, I won't!
He sha'n't see that I mind him, if I burst.

Takes up the vessel again and Exit, looking
back and wiping her eyes.

.

SCENE IV.

The Prison.

CARLO. ANGELICA.

Carlo. And now, dear Angela, for this happy news.
Angel. Thou know'st I told thee of the hundred florins. —
Carlo. Who can it be ? Bertuccio, after all ?
Angel. I went to him. He color'd, but said nothing,
    And steadily refus'd to take them back.
    Last night I found two hundred more, which Gianni
    Had been seduc'd to receive as partial aid
    From friends unknown ('t was thus the message ran.)
    A lady closely veil'd, of noble form,
    And seeming young, and of most gentle speech,
    Deliver'd it, so he said.
        VOL. IV.—15

     Carlo. Perhaps Rugiero,
Bertuccio's son's, young wife.   She 's of the blood,
Thou knowest, of Sozzo Del.
       Angel. It might well be :
But Gianni's prying eyes had found her out.
Some noble friend, more likely, of our cousin's,
Whom he has chosen to mask his generous deed.
Carlo. 'T was nobly done.   I can forgive his fears.
Angel. And now then, Carlo, thou canst leave this den.
  Take Ser Beccari's offer.   For Bertuccio,
We can repay him at our leisure.
       Carlo. How ?
By utter ruin.   Angelica, hear me.   No!
I will not so abuse my sacred trust.
When our dead parents left thee in my hands,
My dearest treasure, as my only joy,
They did not mean, our father could not think,
I should so far forget my honor and them
As for a selfish end, in any way,
To lessen the slender means their woes had left
To keep thee in the state where thou wast born.
'T is little enough as 't is, Heaven knows, to save
That sweet head from depression, and that heart
From disappointment and the natural pang
Of wounded pride.   I will not make it less.
Sell we the farm, the money paid the State,
The palace must be set to public sale.
Forc'd on the mart, 't is little it will bring.
Bertuccio takes three hundred, and the rest

To what land will it bear us ?   Stript of rank,
An exile from thy father's home, reduc'd
To a mere competence or vulgar toil,
Is this the love I promis'd, this the care
Our mother gave thee to ?   Thou shalt not suffer,
Angelica, for my fault.

     Angel. 'T is not thy fault;
'T is Heaven's high will.   What matters where we dwell ?
Art thou not with me ?   Am I not with thee ?
Come, Carlo ! come, my brother ! come, my love !
Is there a place beneath the broad blue Heaven
Shall not be Paradise, so thou art there ?
Is all Siena aught, while thou art here ?

Carlo. O my soul's life ! — But say not, Heaven's will :
Heaven wills not crime. — I have not told thee.   Pon-
  dering,
In my lone hours, these twelve days' dismal past,
It struck me that that bold bad man Beccari,
Having set his heart upon our pretty farm,
Plotted this charge, to force me to his terms.
Why start'st thou, and turn'st pale ?   So think'st thou too ?
Speak, my heart's darling !

     Angel. So I thought but then.
I ——

 Carlo. What hast thou ?   Thou castest down thine eyes.
There is some secret cause why thou so think'st.

Angel. Brother, I meant not to distress thee.   Therefore only
I would not speak.   Be calm.   The Ser Beccari
Offer'd this day to give thee back to freedom

So I would — yield to him my maiden hand.

    CARLO *stands for a moment as if thunderstruck —*
        ANGELICA *gazing on him silently with a*
        look of awe.   Then:

Carlo. This passes all the woes that I have borne.
            Another, but briefer pause.

Lifting solemnly his hands :]

  God, who o'errulest all! canst thou look down
  And see this villain triumph, and his victims,
  His innocent victims stretch their hands in vain ?
      He pauses again briefly, looking earnestly on his
        sister. Then, solemnly, taking her hand ·

Angelica, thou canst not ask me now
To traffic with that man on any terms ;
Not did he offer me ten thousand down !
I am resolv'd. I will not sell the farm.
It is my duty ; and for thy dear sake
Gladly I render up a useless life.
Thou 'lt find with good Bertuccio an asylum.
This he may yield thee easily without fear
Of implication. Nor for aught beside
Shalt thou be owing. The palace and the farm
Will be for thee a dower ——

            Angel. Stop, Carlo, stop!
Hast thou but thought of me, without thyself,
As if I could be separated ? No !
If thou wilt die — I too am ready, I.

The axe indeed will not destroy my life;
But ——

Carlo. [*pressing her closely to his breast.*

Sister! — dearest sister! — Peace! O peace!
Do not speak thus! I yet will think of means.
Yet there is hope; yet, yet. Has not Bertuccio
Provided secretly thus much? Perchance
He will advance the rest a similar way,
And save that sacrifice, which for thy sake,
Thine only, have I shunn'd. — Dry up thy tears —

[*kissing them from her eyes.*

Where now is Barbara? The night comes on.
Angel. I bade her come for me, and wait without.
Carlo. Adieu, now.

[*He taps at the door, which is opened as before.*
Waits the girl there?
Jailer. [*at the sill.*] Yes, Messere.
Angel. [*embracing Carlo passionately — and with broken voice.*
Adieu, my brôther! — Wilt thou? —
Carlo. [*kissing her on the forehead.*] Yes, hope, hope.

[*Exit Angel. and door closes.*

Hope? And when hope is gone, which now fast lessens,
Like the red light of the descended sun,
What then? Shall I bring down that angel nature
Unto a mean condition, to save a life
Which has so little pleasure, and, her except,
No real tie? She will die with me? So
She firmly thinks; but her high moral sense
And trust in God assure her from self-murder,

And the rack'd heart is tougher than she thinks.
And better it is she should remember me
With sorrow and sad love, than see through me
Her scanty means of life made scantier still
To extend my weary being.   Yes! it shall cease.
Forgive me, Heaven, the sin of this deceit;
The sole, I hope, has ever stain'd these lips!

*He leans against the side-scene,
as if looking sadly on the fading twilight, and*

Scene closes.

ACT THE FOURTH

SCENE I. *As in Act I. Sc. II.*

GIACOMO. CAMILLA.

Giac. Thou hast the story now.   Why art thou dumb ?.
    Did I not tell thee, Gasparo would jilt thee ?
Camil. [*with deep expression.*
        He has not done it, though.
                        Giac. No, by St. Paul!
    And shall not!   I have that will bring him straight,
    Were he bent twice as crooked as he is.
Camil. Thou ?   What hast thou to do with it ?   Mind thou,
    Wilt thou, thy own affairs.
                    Giac. I have.   Beccari,
    If he would make a fool of thee. has made
    A —— Hum! —
            Camil. A rogue of thee, thou mean'st.
                            Giac. Thou art,
    Deuse take thee! a shrewd guesser; but thy thoughts
    Go not to the depth of this affair.
                    Camil. What then
    Has Gasparo done to thee?
                    Giac. To me done nothing —
    More than to thee; he has made of me a fool.

But through me has done — what, by St. Paul!
He shall undo, if it should cost me —— [*checks himself.*
   Camil. [*after regarding him*
         fixedly a moment.] Come!
Giacomo dear, dost think Camilla blind,
Because she can be dumb at times? Thou 'rt seldom
Cheerful or complaisant ——
         Giac. Don't mince it; say
I am moody and harsh-spoken; and I am.
God knows I have cause! My cursed luck —— What
   then?
Camil. These three days past, thou hast been much more than
   moody,
Savage in thy moroseness; thy fierce eyes,
Sullen and bloodshot, dart at times strange fire,
And thy clench'd hands keep motion with thy lips,
Which fold on one another as thy teeth
Gnash in thy passion, and thy lowering brows
Are knit together. Often too by night ——
Giac. Wilt thou have done? curse on thee! Are my veins
Swollen with water, that I should know thy wrongs,
And feel I am too far bounden to Beccari
To dare resent them; am I less, I say,
Or more than man that I should brook this insult,
And not be tortur'd?
      Camil. Am I less than woman,
That I may not be trusted to avenge
My own hurt pride? If 't is not water swells
Thy veins, good brother, mine are not of milk.

The same blood boils beneath my softer skin
As flushes thine; and, credit me, my nerves
Give quite as keen perception.   So, I say,
'T is not alone my wrongs, but something more
Rouses the tiger of thy savage mood.
" Done *through* thee ? — what he shall undo ? "
                                         What 's that ?
Let the beast sleep again, or make me know,
Who was whelp'd with thee, what the blood thou snuff'st
In the tainted air ?
   Giac. [*with his usual scoffing laugh.*
                         Thy metaphors are choice.
It is the tiger, is it not, that lurks
For innocent blood ?   Curse on the knave Beccari !
     He takes a step or two, to and fro,
      CAMILLA *watching him steadily from under her brows.*
I 'll tell thee thus much.   Messer Provenzano
Salvani, who, some fifty years ago,
Was Governor in Siena, and himself
Did much what Messer Gasparo Beccari
As a ninth part of the government now would do,
Being told by the Devil his head should be the highest
Of all the host at the battle of Valdelsa,
Thought he should conquer, and —— Thou hast heard
    the tale.
Camil. The Florentines cut off his head and bore it
    On a lance's point over all the field.[27]   What next ?
Giac. Where is thy "keen perception ? "   'T is the Devil
    Dupes the ninth fraction of the government now.
    15*

He may give his head for another's : that is all.

Camil. Thou hast said enough to damn thee, brother Giacomo,
Say'st thou not more.   Say on.

      Giac. Could I but trust thee !
O ! it were such relief to uncloak this secret
Which gnaws into my vitals ! to obtain
The assistance of thy cunning to o'erreach him,
And save the innocent blood !

      Camil. The innocent blood ?
Has he then tempted thee to do a murder ?
Or does it through thee ?

  Giacomo *walks apart, with signs of violent emotion.*

      — But it is thy secret.
Thou need'st not tell it.   I have heard enough.
Only —— [*affecting to go.*
 Giac. 'T is better to tell all, or none :
This thou wouldst say.   'T is right.   Camilla, stop !
Time presses : what I would do, must be done
On the instant. [*Pauses and grasps her hand.*
    Messer Carlo Montanino ——

  Giacomo *stops.*   Camilla, *gazing a moment on*
   his working features, suddenly flings off his
     hand with horror.

Camil. — This day must suffer on an unprov'd charge.
I see it all !   Wast thou the accursed wretch
That swore away his innocent life ?   For what ?
That from his ruin the fiend of Hell, Beccari,

Might put another in thy sister's place?
Was it for money thou didst it?   Doubly Judas!
Go buy a cord, and hang thyself: thou art not
Fit to live. [*Goes up the stage towards the door.*

    Giac. Camilla! — Woman! — Stop! [26]
Think'st thou to carry it thus?   My heart 's as strong,
Or stronger than thy own; my will shall be
Quite as imperious, if thou mak'st me use
The rights I have by nature and by justice.
Justice, I say.   What! darest thou to believe
I sold the Montanino's blood?   First, hear me;
Then play the tyrant.   The hell-knave, Beccari,
Made me to think it was but Carlo's farm
He coveted, and, pandering to my wants,
Craftily brib'd me to that step should force him
To sell 't.   I had no thought — thou shalt not think it!
To put his life in peril.   And now I go
To save it at the peril of my own.

Camil. Stop thou in turn.   This is all true?

                  Giac. By Heaven!
Tak'st thou me for a villain unredeem'd,
Like thy damn'd suitor, because I have given my soul
To the hell-lust of gaming?   Thou shalt see.

                  [*again turning to go.*

Camil. What wilt thou do?

             Giac. Go straightway to the tempter,
And force him on the instant pay the fine,
Or at once hand him over, and myself,
To the tribunal.

Camil. And thus ruin both. —
What dost thou owe him ?

   Giac. Five hundred florins.

     Camil. The wretch !
He had set his heart indeed upon 't, to bribe
So largely.

  Giac. 'T is my debt entire.

     Camil. No matter
How vilely 't was incurr'd, thou ow'st it ; he
His hand to me. Accuse him, and thou losest
Thy sister's husband, and thyself must pay ——
How wilt thou pay it ?

    Giac. O devil ! there 's the chain
Has bound me to his enginery !

     Camil. I 'll file it,
And with the servant set the victim free.

Giac. Servant ? Thou 'rt bitter ! Let it pass. But him !
How wilt thou do it ?

    Camil. Leave that to me. Enough,
Thou hast my word. I 'll do it.

    Giac. But on the instant !
Goes the sun down, the penalty unpaid ——
There 's but an hour now left !

    Camil. It is enough :
Gasparo will be here within ten minutes.

Giac. And thou wilt save young Montanino ? Swear it !

Camil. I swear it by high Heaven ! He shall not die.

Giac. [*exultingly.*

He shall not die ! — But work thou well, and quickly.

l go to the Place, to wait the fatal hour.

If the bell toll and Carlo be led forth,

I 'll shout my guilt in public, and the axe,

If fall it must, shall fall on me, not him.

Camil. It shall not need: nor his blood, nor thy own

    Shall fleck the sand. I swear it! Go in peace.

Giac. O what a load is off my breast! I breathe.

    I do not smell of blood now. Let me hug thee.

    'T is the first time I 've done it since I was man.

    He shall not die! Thou 'lt save him! Thou wilt save him!

                                  [*Exit Giac.*

    Camilla *looks after him thoughtfully a moment, then,*

        with brows knitted and hands clenched:

Camil. Yes, I will save him. But not as thou dost think.

    I 'll save him by the law. This villain Gasparo

    Shall not wrong *me.* — My brother is involv'd.

    What then? Shall I be balk'd of my revenge?

    Shall Justice too be thwarted in her right

    Because of kin? He has sown: so let him reap.

    It shall avail to mitigate his punishment

    That he has sought to save the Montanino,

    And had no thought to bring him unto death.

                [*Goes rapidly up to the door,*

        and Scene closes.

·

Scene II.

In the Palazzo Salimbeni.
Ippolito's Cabinet.

Ippolito *before a table on which stands a*
casket, apparently of oak, richly
carved in half-relief.

Ippol. The hour approaches.   There is left no time
   To think what should be, or of other plans
   Might stead him better, were there only time
   To shape and weigh them.   It is wondrous strange
   Angelica's brother should set less by life
   Than fortune.   Young, and capable, with life,
   He might redeem it; but —— Why! none but fools,
   Grown desperate, fling away both end and means,
   And, in a sort of childish spite with fortune,
   Will none of life because they cannot hold it
   On their own terms!   He is no wayward child,
   No moody lack-brain.   They who know him best
   Make him high-minded, resolute, severe,
   With an exalted fancy that exaggerates
   The claims of love and duty, and a sense
   Of honor like a Roman's of old time,
   Ere Rome was yet an Emperor's or a Pope's.
   He has some serious aim.   His known devotion
   To his young sister, — and even for that my heart,
   For that, yearns towards him —— Ay! it must be so!

He means upon the altar of his love
To offer his young life ! Thou self-bound Isaac !
There shall not want a ram to take thy place !
These idle ducats ——

    About to open the casket, pauses, and
       turns round again.

    But what will he think ?
What will the world think ? Think I mean to shame him,
Bound with the fetters of a twofold debt,
Of money and life, to his ancestral foe.
Or haply —— No ! that were a villain's thought,
Not Montanino's. No ! Think what he will,
He shall not think me heartless, as his friends
And mother's kin have prov'd. And thou, Angelica ! ——

    Unlocks and proceeds to open the casket
       as Scene closes.

SCENE III.

The Prison.

CARLO.   ANGELICA.

BARBARA *near the door.*

Angel. No hope! no hope! The hour draws nigh! My brother!
   My brother, on my knees, [*kneeling and embracing his knees.*
                    I pray have pity,
   Have pity on thyself alike and me.
Carlo. [*endeavoring to raise her.*
   It is, Angelica, that I have pity,
   Have pity on myself alike and thee,
   I am thus stubborn.   Wouldst thou have me live
   To see thee less than Nature made thee be,
   And Heaven ordain'd?
                    Angel. I never shall be less,
   Be what I may, than Heaven did ordain.
   Has thou not heard, that to the fleeceless lamb
   The wind is temper'd?
                    Carlo. But the shepherd sees
   A murrain thin his flock, nor does the wolf
   Flesh his sharp tooth the less because his prey
   Is undefended.   In Bertuccio's fold,
   Thy guarded fleece will keep its silky flocks
   Safe from the wayside briers of the world.
   Rise up, fair lamb.

Angel. No; here I rest. Is this,
Carlo, is this thy promise? Thou didst say
Thou 'dst think of other means. Thou bad'st me hope.
Thou mad'st me think thou 'dst seek for other aid
From good Bertuccio. But for this, myself,
Myself had sought it, begg'd it on my knees.

Carlo. And begg'd in vain.

       Angel. As I do now — for mercy;
For mercy, cruel Carlo, for myself,
From thee, my only brother, who I thought
Once lov'd me only.

       Carlo. Once? Once lov'd thee? Once?
Is my blood — must I say it? — which I pour
Freely —— O never pagan priest yet pour'd
From the bound victim's veins a freer stream,
Than that I scatter gladly from my own
For thy sole sake! ——

       Angel. It is not thy own blood;
It is our father's. In thy single stem
Flows all the sap of our three-hundred years.
What right hast thou to let it out at once,
And raze the Montanino to the ground?
Last scion of the parent tree, stand up,
And wave thy yet green boughs, and blossom still,
As God commands!

       Carlo. Angelica! cease! cease!
Make not what I deem'd virtue seem a crime :·
Call not our father's spirit to the block;
Name me not parricide of all my race.

Thou art my sister, and shouldst smooth that way
I thought to tread so lightly, and must tread.
'T is now too late.   See there ! [*pointing off the scene as to*
the setting sun.

                 Angel. 'T is not too late ! [*start-*
ing to her feet.

Let me go, brother !   Do not hold me !
                 Carlo. Go ?

Whither?   Before thou reach——   *Suddenly.*] Yes, go ;
go quickly.   [*kissing her passionately, and straining*
her in his embrace.

Angel. [*takes both his hands in hers, and looking him steadily*
in the face, and with solemnity.

Carlo, my brother, thou hast deceiv'd me once :
'T was the sole falsehood ever stain'd thy lips.
Thou mean'st to spare me now the final pang,
And have no parting.   Is it so?
    The bolts of the door are heard to be withdrawn.
                 What 's that? [*wildly.*

They are come ! they are come to fetch thee ! O my God !
       hanging on him with both arms — but her eyes
       straining fixed upon the door,

           which opens, and

    Enter, unattended, the CAPTAIN *of the Guard.*

          BARBARA *comes forward.*

Capt. It is my happiness to inform Messere,
The penalty is paid, and he is free.

ANGELICA, *relaxing her hold,*
falls without a sound into the arms of BARBARA.

Carlo. By whom?   Who is it?

       Capt. I know not.   This is all.

        [*pointing to the warrant*
         which he holds open.

Carlo. Bertuccio!   How shall we? —— Angelica! [*turning*
          rapidly.

        Hear'st thou?

Capt. Messer', she has fainted from excess of joy.

  CARLO *takes* ANGELICA *in his arms.*

BARBARA *goes hastily to a water-jug which stands on a table in*
the background, and is seen coming forward with it, —
the JAILER *advancing a step into the cell, and the* CAPTAIN
standing by ANGELICA'S *feet with a look of respectful*
sympathy, — as

the Drop falls. .

ACT THE FIFTH

SCENE I.   *As in Act I. Scene IV.*

CARLO.   ANGELICA.

BARBARA — *in the act of leaving :*
ANGELICA *looking towards her, as waiting her departure ;*
CARLO, *with arms folded and eyes on the ground.* — *Exit* BARBARA.

Angel. And now, my brother. [*Carlo takes her hand and gazes
earnestly and mournfully in her face.*
But thou seem'st not glad.
Carlo. [*after a moment's silence — still gazing on her.*
No, I am sore oppress'd.   Though free, I am bound;
Bounden forever, save thou loose the chain.
Angel. What canst thou mean ?   How deadly pale thou look'st!
Carlo. It is my desperate purpose makes me pale,
And the long pang it cost me to resolve.
Angel. I heard thee pace thy chamber to and fro,
And wonder'd, Carlo, what should make thee linger,
Knowing my longing to receive thy news.
Carlo. And when thou hear'st it ! ——
[*He pauses and again looks her gravely in the face.*
Angel. Hast thou seen him ?
Carlo. Whom?
Angel. Our cousin, surely.   Was 't not Arrigucci

Thou went'st to see? thy saviour, Carlo — mine?

Carlo. Would that he were! I were then less perplex'd.

I saw him not.   There was no need.   Last night,

When Arrigucci came not, though I felt

'T was modesty perhaps that kept him back

When others wish'd me joy, who was the source

Of our great happiness, or fear again

To be committed with the tyrannous Nine,

Yet — thou hast heard me say — my mind misgave me,

And better seem'd it me to wait till morn,

Till the fisc open'd, to learn who really was

My generous liberator. —

> *Angel. [who has listen'd full of wonderment,*
>   *now eagerly.*

>   And thou hast learn'd?

Carlo. [*his eyes still fixed on Angel.*

The Chancellor told me Salimbene's self,

Ippolito Salimbene paid the fine,

With his own hand.   Why how thou pal'st, my sister!

And now, thy face is burning! while thine eyes

Gleam satisfaction through their tears!

> [*Angel. throws herself on his neck and hides her confusion.*

>   Is 't so?

Wouldst thou then rather it were Salimbene

Than Arrigucci?

> *Angel. [lifting her head instantly.*

>   No, no, Carlo, no!

Rather 't were almost any one than he.

Carlo. And so would I.

Angel. Yet 't was a noble act.

Carlo. Ay, truly so! My enemy did for me
    What none of my friends would do; the heir of those
    Who spent my father's race, lifts up from death
    The last male scion of that hated stock,
    Which, dead in me, would never more put forth
    Or fruit or flower to bear the hostile name.
    'T would wash him snow-white, were he spotted o'er
    With twice two centuries of my foresires' blood!

            [*Angel. looks admiringly through her tears.*

    How well that dew becomes thee! Dry it not;
    Such Heaven sprinkles on its angels' eyes
    When they applaud in silence good men's deeds;
.   And such is Salimbene. O my sister!
    I fear thou wilt shed other tears anon,
    Bitter as these are sweet.

            Angel. What 's on thy heart?

Carlo. The weight of obligation, which makes dull
    Its glad pulsations. How shall we repay him?

Angel. With our life's service.

            Carlo. Even so I mean:
    And that in earnest. [*with same expression — regarding
               her fixedly.*

            Art thou then prepar'd
    To be his servitor, as I shall be?

Angel. What means that emphasis? Why that fixed look?
    Speak out thy purpose, brother.

            Carlo. Salimbene
    Loves thee, my sister. -- Over all thy face

The rose supplants the lily.   'T is the hue
Not of displeasure, Angela; and my heart
Trembles to feel the sacrifice it makes
May be to thee too easy.

     Angel. What is that?
Why shouldst thou think that Salimbene ——
       [*embarrassed.*] Why,
Why with imputed selfishness·of thought
Stain his brave action?

     Carlo. 'T is not to be selfish
To owe the impulsion to a generous deed
To some deep-cherish'd feeling.   No base love
Prompts to great action, and an enemy's life
Sav'd to win favor in the sister's heart
Is still high inspiration.   Salimbene
Loves thee, Angelica, and for thee alone
Has done thus bravely.   'T is with thee alone
I can repay him.

     Angel. Carlo! — Dost thou think? ——
Carlo. Of the wide gulf which Fortune spreads between
Our state and his?   I do.   But for that gulf
I were not now his debtor for my life.
Well do I know 't is not for me to offer
What, were we even equals, he should beg.
'T is not thy hand, my sister.   Said I not
We are his slaves?   And slaves are handed over
Without condition.

     Angel. Speak not so dejectly.
And speak less darkly, brother.   I but feel

Thou hast some solemn purpose, whose sad thought
I read in thy pale visage and chang'd eye,
But cannot give it shape.

     Carlo. I would thou couldst!
So were I spar'd some anguish.

      Angel. O my heart!
What canst thou mean then?

      Carlo. Part we with our all,
Thou wouldst be there wherefrom to rescue thee
I would have given my life, would give it still.
But, could I do this, should I have the right,
For Salimbene's sake?

     Angel. No, Carlo, no!
'T would seem like flinging back the hand he tenders
In amity, it may be in atonement
Of our ancestral wrongs.

     Carlo. I think not so:
The wrong was what our sires had done to his,
Had they been strong enough.   Still, thus to act
Would seem indeed like o'erstrain'd pride, or rancor.
We cannot so repay him.   I must give
That which alone he covets, my sole treasure.
It is thyself, my sister, and, alas!
Without condition.

    Angel. Thou dost mean?

      Carlo His slave,
To make my sister too his handmaid.

      Angel. Never!
'T is not my brother! not my father's son!

Not Carlo Montanino, speaks!

    Carlo. [*mournfully*] Angelica,

Look on me. Need I ? ——

        Angel. [*who has gone from him a step*
        indignantly, returning and throwing herself,
        weeping, on his neck.

        No! remind me not!

Thou wouldst have given thy life for me. And now,

Wouldst thou make vile and cast away forever

What was so precious ? Sorrow, and anxious thought,

And prison-solitude, have made thee wild.

Thou wilt sleep over this, and waken calmer.

Carlo. I have slept over it, and I am calm. —

Listen, my sister, — precious to me now

More than thou ever wast, if love like mine

Admit of increase. We had thought it much,

Had Arrigucci privily lent us aid.

But Salimbene, openly and bravely

Like a true man, and in the cause of right,

Exerts his sympathy, and defies the Nine,

Scorning their verdict. We had ow'd him much,

Had he through others but spent on us that sum.

But thus to take me boldly by the hand

As though I were a brother, to lift me up

When others durst not look on me, to give me

The life that but for him were gone forever,

This noble friend, this more to me than brother,

This re-creator, what then shall repay him ?

Angel. Carlo! my brother!

    Vol. IV.—16

Carlo. — Not my life alone.
That were not to give all I have, not give
What is most precious in his eyes, and mine.
But if I bid him take that for which only
Life to me is worth living ——

         Angel. Brother! brother!
Son of my father! who art in his place, —
      [sinking on her knees before him.
Give not to infamy thy orphan charge!
Sell all thou hast, let us be poor and outcast.
I can even serve, if needful; but not here —
Not him — not Salimbene!

        Carlo. Be 't as thou wilt.
One way remains: it cancels not our debts,
But makes us not to feel them.   Rise, my sister.
       [endeavoring to raise her.
Angel. Carlo! wouldst break my heart?

        Carlo. Oh Salimbene!
Hadst thou but loiter'd in thy work of love
All were now over, by a death that seem'd
Noble as martyrdom! but now no thought
Of sacrifice for duty lifts the soul,
And death's sharp agony will have tenfold horror
In that 'tis but the severance from shame!
Angel. Death! And is that thy meaning?

       Carlo. And what else
Will lift from me the load I cannot bear?
Angel. *[rising quickly.*
    Then let us die together.   Better thus

Than live the death of infamy.   Salimbene,
Bequeath'd our heritage, will be more than paid.

Carlo. Of infamy, sister?   Hast thou then believ'd
That such I offer'd?   I? to thee?   Thou heard'st me:
Never base love yet prompted generous deed ;
And such was Salimbene's.   When in anguish
To be so fetter'd, knowing no escape
Save death from obligation, the dread thought
Flash'd like the thunder through my prison'd soul,
To give for all he had given the all I had —
All he could value, — when this lurid light
Burst on the darkness of my spirit and shook me
With fears that made my very flesh to creep
With a cold shivering, — though it show'd the way
To instant freedom, I had shut my eyes
Sitting still fetter'd, had not reason show'd
My fears were idle, and call'd the warm glow back
To my chill'd skin.   It was a mortal ague, [*shuddering.*
But it is over ; though I still am pale.

Angel. Ay, deadly pale, my brother ; and should be.
Fi on this madness!   It is such: no reason
Counsels dishonor ; and that wholesome terror
That made thy man's-pulse throb, and thy warm blood
That is so valiant chilly, trust it! 't was
The appeal of God, thy conscience ; trust it, Carlo !

Carlo. Thou wilt not hear me.   I would say : — I thought,
And reason'd with my terror ; and my blood
Ran free again.   For well I grew assur'd
That Salimbene would but do as I

In a like case, and rather make addition
Unto his noble act, than dim its splendor
By even thought of evil.

        Angel. Then to offer
Were but deceit. O Carlo, be thyself!
Let not misfortune warp thy simple faith!

Carlo. It has not, sister. When I give thee up,
My sole possession that has any worth
In Salimbene's eyes, my all in mine,
The sacrifice is perfect and sincere.
The sense that he will not misuse the gift,
The knowledge that his nature cannot be
Both mean and generous, noble and debas'd,
Strip it of all its terror and half its pain,
But leave the act still thorough. Thou art his
Without condition, subject to his will.

Angel. [*once more falling at his feet.*
Thou wilt not do it! Thou art still my brother!
Thou wilt not soil our father's fame, and mine.
O say thou wilt not!

        Carlo. Not in any way.
Nor give thee up against thy will. Be tranquil:
My debt shall rest unpaid. [*Raises her.*

        Angel. But then? — But then?—
Thou dost not mean? —— Thou wilt — do nothing des·
perate?

    She holds both his hands in hers. — He releases one,
        and lays it on her shoulder.

Carlo. Angelica, were my simple service, vow'd

For life to my life's creditor, enough,
Or could I earn by any kind of work
Sufficient to repay him, it were well.
But there is no resource for me in toil,
And **my** sole servitude would be disclaim'd,
And, offer'd solely, seem a mere pretence,
So certain its rejection.   Shall I then
Skulk in the noontide by my enemy's door,
Or cower when we meet, his hopeless debtor?
My days are melancholy now enough,
With even thy sunshine over me; but then!
In the bleak shadow of a fix'd despair,
Dead to myself and thee!   I should go mad.
Would that the axe had fallen in time!

Angel. Hush! hush!

Thou wouldst have given thy life for me : not now
Through me shall that dear life be darken'd over,
By even a passing shadow of despair.
With Heaven to aid me, I will do thy bidding.

Carlo. No, no, not mine! not mine!   Do thy own will.

Angel. And that shall be thy bidding, — ever, Carlo.
Is sacrifice for thee alone?   Shall I
Not there too be thy sister?   That poor station
Thou wouldst have steadied with thy corpse, I now,
To keep thee living, step from, and — Oh God!
Must it so be, will peril even maiden fame.

Carlo. Think not so meanly of our generous saviour.
Thou wilt see, Angela, all will yet be well.

Angel. I hope so: yet I fear.   Should he — abuse

The gift which —— Hark! I will not live.

         Carlo. Nor I.

We both will go down to our father's tomb.
And better so, if Salimbene's soul
Can so defile itself: this world is then
Not worth the living in, and thou and I
Were better out of it. —— But think on this.
To-morrow ——

    Angel. No, no! take me now, at once.
Give not a moment! for — I dare not think.

Falls on his neck.   He presses her soothingly to his breast.

Scene closes.

Scene II.

Same as in Act II. Scene I.

Ippolito.   Cornelia.   Domicilla.

Domicil. Well, I 'm not sorry — nay, I am heartily **glad**
   The young man is at large.   It had been cruel
   To cut his head off for so small a crime;

Although, the Montanino is no friend
Of ours ——
    Ippol. But may be soon. [*looking significantly at*
                                   Cornelia.
            Domicil. Why, how thou talk'st !
In my day —— But I should be glad to know
Who paid that fine. 'T is very odd ! That Nello,
I'm sure, knows more than he cares tell. " A noble
And brave cavalier" [*reflectingly.*] —— No doubt ! He must
Have been a bold one. [*Cornelia looks attentively at*
                   Ippol., who smiles.
            But 't is surely odd
His name should not be known. I 'll have the rogue
Come up again.
    Ippol. [*stopping her as she turns, apparently to*
            touch a handbell.
        Nay, aunt, 't is not worth while :
It all must soon be out. And here, in fact,
Comes the rogue's self.

       Enter ANTONELLO.

       Domicil. Now, Nello ——
             Anton. Pardon, madam :
          [*then turning directly to Ippol.*
Ser Carlo Montanino with a lady
Waits in the hall, and humbly craveth audience
Alone of the Messere.

Ippol. [*with agitation.*] With a lady?

Domicil. [*who has been dumb with amazement.*

  The Montanino in my father's halls!

And humbly craves! Thou wilt not surely see him?

Ippol. Why not?

   Domicil. Alone?

     Ippol. No, with a lady. Aunt,

Thee and Cornelia I must pray retire. —

To Nello.] Say to the noble gentleman, myself

Will wait on him immediately. [*Exit Anton.*

    Domicil. [*retiring.*] What next?

The Montanino sues the Salimbene!

In his own hall! and humbly! Times *are* chang'd.

Heaven keep us! Come, Cornelia. [*Exit.*

   Cornel. [*putting her hand in her brother's with*

      an admiring and affectionate look.

        Dear Ippol'to!

It was then thou?

  Ippol. [*smiling.*] Didst thou not show the way?

   Exit CORNELIA *after* DOMICILLA,

 while IPPOLITO *turns to the other side of the scene,*

  but hesitating as he is about to leave.

A lady! — Angel'? —— Too late! [*Stands aside,*

    bowing profoundly, as

  Enter CARLO, *leading* ANGELICA *veiled.*

   CARLO, *who is deadly pale,*

returning the salutation with an air of deep submission,

 speaks with a melancholy yet dignified humility.

Carlo. Messere, pardon.

It was not meet that you, who are henceforth
My lord forever, should descend to me,
Your servant. I have therefore rather chosen
To venture uninvited to your presence. —
Ippol. Messer', the honor that you do this roof ——
Carlo. My lord, pray pardon me again. Such terms
Are not for you to me. What you have done ——
Ippol. Ah, pardon me in turn. I have been bold ;
But only as, I think, you would have been
Under like circumstance : you must excuse me.
Will you be seated ?

       Carlo. It is not fit for us. —
Be not amaz'd, but hear me. What I owe
I have no means to render, only one.
You are the master of my life ; I am
The humblest of your bondsmen, ready ever
To do your sternest bidding without stop.
But that is not enough. I have one gift
You will more value.

    ANGELICA, *who has hitherto*
leaned drooping on her brother's right shoulder,
now grasps his arm in both her hands,
her head hanging down over them,
and seems ready to sink.

      Could the Almighty God
Of all this world but give me once the choice
16*

To be so blest as I have been in her,

> [*freeing his right arm, while raising her with the other,*
>> *he puts his right hand on her head.*

Or be the lord of all in proud Siena,
I would take poverty again and this　.
His angel; for she is my heart, my brain;
There is no other like to her on earth.
Yet, being such, I give her.　She is yours.

> [*He throws back Angelica's veil.*

I need not say to you who are so noble,
Be kind to her; you will not use her ill.
And now, permit me.　[*Putting out his hand to Ippolito,*
> *while Angelica, unsupported sinks into a chair.*

> IPPOLITO *mistaking the action,*
> *and still in the extremity of surprise, mechanically*
> *extends his own, to meet his grasp.　But* CARLO, *taking it*
> *by the fingers respectfully, raises it, in the*
> *manner of an inferior and dependent, to his lips, and*
> *immediately, with the same melancholy humbleness, without*
> *looking at his sister, Exit.*
> ANGELICA *puts out one of her hands,*
> *as if to arrest him, then, recollecting herself, sinks*
> *back in the chair, and covers her face with*
> *both hands, weeping, while* IPPOLITO *stands confounded*
> *before her.　At length rousing himself.*

> *Ippol.* Lady, do not fear. [*tremulously.*

I — go to bring those to you from whose lips

You will more readily learn than mine, that here
You have but to command.   But first that homage,
Your brother in my moment of surprise
Made me receive, let me return to you.
My heart goes with it.

> *He kneels, and with reverence, yet with evident*
> *emotion, raises her hand to his lips.*

Angel. Messere — O believe ! ——
[*bursts into tears.*

Ippol. I do believe — I know — why you are here.
The sacrifice is holy, is heroic,
And lifts you higher, were there greater height,
In my esteem.   But that I deem it were
To insult the helpless state wherein your brother
Through a too lofty spirit and pride has plac'd you,
I would here tell you how I have long lov'd,
Ador'd you.   Only from the fear to offend
Both you and him, have I not ventur'd ever
More than an outward reverence — and perhaps
The homage of my eyes.   O could I think ! ——

> *She weeps, and does not withdraw her hand.*

Yes, yes, thou doubt'st me not ; thou knowest, thou feelest,
Feel'st in thy own pure spirit, I could not dream
To impose on thy position.   Let me then,
Ere come my aunt, and sister, who has known
From the very first my love, and learn'd to love thee,

Say all.   Angelica! at thy maiden feet
Ippolito lays his fortune, honor, name.
If thou disdain them not, say but one word,
But one, and make them thine.

> *Angel.* [*with mingled joy and ten-*
> *derness, as she hides her blushes on his shoulder.*

Ippolito!—

Scene closes.

SCENE III. AND THE·LAST.

As in Act I. Scene I.

CARLO

seated at a table near the centre, his face hidden in his
hands, the fingers of which are buried in his hair.
After some moments,
Enter BARBARA *from the left.*
She moves a step or two towards him, then stoops
and curtsies several times, pausing a little after each inclination.

She approaches then nearer, so as to attract his attention,
and again curtsies — his back being towards her.

Carlo. [*half turning his head, then resuming his attitude.*
What want'st thou, girl?
       Barb. Where is Madonna, Master?
Carlo. [*dropping his hands, but without looking at her,*
    and speaking slowly and with great mournfulness.
Where? — Where? — I would I knew!
        Barb. O God, Messere!
Do not speak so! you frighten me.
        Carlo. I meant not.
Thy mistress is not here. Go seek her. [*sadly, but without*
            harshness.
        Barb. Gianni
Knows where she is, but will not tell me.
        Carlo. Gianni
Knows nothing, more than I. He saw me lead her
Out to the street, and whither. Where — and what ——
Go to thy chamber; thou wilt know to-morrow.
Go to thy chamber, girl.

BARBARA *is about to retire, but stops suddenly by the*
embrasure of a window in the left wing, and appears to look out.
CARLO, *hearing her stop, turns round.*

Seriously, but still without harshness.
       What mak'st thou there
At the window, girl? Didst thou not hear me? Go.
Barb. Pardon, Messere; there. is something doing

At the Palazzo Salimbeni yon. [*looking eagerly again.*
Carlo. [*springing up.*

Ah! Mercy, God! — What seest thou?

Barb. People standing
At the great gate. There 's something to come out.
Carlo. [*motionless in the centre — seemingly arrested by terror.*

And? —— Look again, good Barba. Seem they sad?
Barb. No, merry. Hear their murmurs! Look, dear Master.
Carlo. I cannot look. [*Barb. gazing with increased earnestness.*

— What now?

Barb. It is — Giesù!
Madonna's self! with Messer Salimbene!
She looks so happy! though her eyes are down —
And blushes scarlet. One hand is in his,
The other holds in hers Madonna Nelia,
And Monna Domicilla walks beside.

CARLO *clasps his hands in ecstasy, but*
stands as before.

They 're coming hither! How the people shout!
Now Monna Nelia whispers something low,
. Which makes Madonna smile, but blush still more;
And Messer Salimbene scatters gold,
Which the rogues gather up, first shouting louder.
They 're in!

She starts from the window, and without regarding
her master, runs across the stage.

— I knew! I knew! O happy day!

[*Exit at the right.*
Carlo. [*who, tottering backward, has sunk into the chair.*

I thank Thee, Heaven! And pardon me my doubts!

After a few moments,

he appears to recover, and resuming his wonted majesty of mien,

moves slowly to the right, where presently

Enter

ANGELICA, IPPOLITO, CORNELIA, *and* DOMICILLA,

bowed in by GIANNI, *and followed by* BARBARA.

ANGELICA *rushes into* CARLO'S *arms.*

Angel. Brother!

Carlo. My darling! and my life! — Messere,

I crave your pardon; and yours, noble ladies,

That I have made your welcome wait; but joy

In this recover'd treasure ——

Ippol. Which is mine.

Revoke not, Messer Carlo. What you gave

I come now to accept, not to restore.

For Carlo's sister is now Ippolito's bride.

[*raises Angelica's hand to his lips.*

Carlo. Noble Ippolito! you have crush'd with debt

Your poor but happy debtor. Half my gift

Has Angela taken away, to give, herself.

The other yet remains; for I am still,

As I shall ever be, your humblest bondsman,

Ready to do your bidding as my lord.

GIANNI, *in the background, betrays consternation,*

and BARBARA *surprise.* DOMICILLA *gazes on* CARLO *with wonder*

and interest, and CORNELIA *with admiration.*

Ippol. You hear him, all?

Gianni. [*muttering.*] His grandsire would have heard
An earthquake sooner; that is my idea.

Domicil. And mine, old man.   The times are sorely chang'd.

Ippol. And thou shalt change too, Aunt.

                    Carlo. [*severely.*] Be silent, Gianni.
The Salimbene's love would fill these walls,
Though they were left still emptier than they are
By Montaninan hatred.

                    Ippol. Nobly said!
Is 't not, Cornelia? [*looking closely at his sister, who has
                    manifested some emotion.*

                    Carlo, thou hast said
Thou 'lt do my bidding.

                    Carlo. [*solemnly.*] Truly, in all things.

Ippol. Make suit then to my sister.   Unto her
I here transfer thy service.   Canst thou win her,
Thou 'lt win what 's worth the wearing, and render me,
Doubly thy brother, lighter i' the conscience,
As having made restitution for this treasure
Whereof I 've robb'd thee. [*drawing Angel. lightly to him.*

    Carlo. [*seizing his hand.*] Generous Salimbene!

Domicil. Now Heaven help us!

                    Carlo. [*turning to Cornelia with mod-
                    esty, yet with dignity.*

                    Lady, if such as I,
A man so fallen in fortune and sad of heart,
Venture to lift his thoughts to such as you,
Whom under luckier stars he had been happy
And proud to dare address, ascribe it kindly

Not to too forward a spirit, but duty vow'd
To my life's master.

    Cornel. Sir, must I make answer?
I rate so high my brother's love for me,
I cannot think he would have chosen else
Than for my happiness; and he whose life
Was freely offer'd for his sister's sake,
And whom that sister better lov'd than fame,
Lifts not his thoughts, but lowers, to such as I. —

Ippol. [*half aside to Carlo.*
  Is she not worthy?

    Cornel. [*continuing.*] If my aunt approve ——

Domicil. That word redeems us all. In my day, maidens ——

Ippol. Had hearts of just such pliant stuff as now;
  And Monna Domicilla was but woo'd
  As Angela and Cornelia must be won.

Domicil. Child, thou forgott'st me.

    Ippol. No, I but forestall'd:
I knew beforehand what thou wouldst approve.

Domicil. [*to Carlo.*] Sir, I am yet too much a Salimbene
  To say that I rejoice; but this believe:
  I truly honor you, and one day may love.

Ippol. [*hugging her, —'she struggling in his arms, half pleased,
  half piqued.*
  Why, that's my aunt! I said that thou wouldst change.

Carlo. [*kissing her hand.*] Madonna, I shall strive to win your
  favor;
  And hope to, will this lady teach me how.

Ippol. [*to Cornel., as Carlo kisses her hand in turn.*

Cornelia's ring, thou seest, is soon reset.

Cornel. With such another jewel as the first.

Ippol. But burn'd a deeper sanguine in the fire
      Which has not tried the ruby of my love.

Cornel. I 'll wear them, brother; both then, side by side.

Ippol. First ask Angelica.   Half my heart, I said,
      Was long since hers.

> *Cornel.* And half of Messer Carlo's
      Is still his sister's.   Thus I have but one.
      And thou, Angelica, art not better off.
      These men are but half lovers.

> *Angel.* But these brothers!

Cornel. Ah! there, Angelica, both of us agree.
      We 'll keep each other's brother; and they shall see
      Which half is better set, with thee or me.

GIANNI, *who has been curiously watching Cornelia, and working
      himself more and more forward, now advancing to Carlo.*

Gianni. That is the lady, Master, I 'm a-thinking,
      That left the roll of florins at the gate.
      And the same too gave Barbara the hundred;
      That 's my idea.

      Barb. [*to Angel.*] Madonna, pardon me.
      The secret now is told; but [*to Cornel.*] not through me.

Carlo. And to our enemies we thus owe all!
      O lady, can my life, which you would ransom,
      And your brave brother, my true lord, has redeem'd,
      Ever repay these benefits from both?
      So let me be indeed thy servitor,

And all the idolatry I paid my sister
Shall henceforth yield its worship at thy shrine.
> [*kisses Cornel.'s hand with evident emotion.*

Domicil. [*with tender reproach.*

Couldst thou not, niece, have let me share in this ? —

Cornel. Dear aunt, I fear'd — thou knowest, thy family
views ——

Domicil. Naughty Cornelia! was I so mistrusted ?

But I won't contradict: for, in my day,
Such things were never thought of. Well! I hope
'T is for the better; but 't is true the times
Are sadly chang'd.

> *Ippol.* No, gladly, say, my aunt.

Domicil. Don't contradict me, dear my boy.

> *Ippol.* No, aunt:

For here are foes no more to breed dispute.
The Montanino-Salimbene one,
Thou shalt have care henceforth alone to see
Times change indeed, but let them still agree.

BARBARA,

who after her brief part in the colloquy has been seen to
go to the window, and there respond by sign to some signal from
without, and then steal off from the scene, now re-enters,
leading in ANTONELLO. *Both appear excited.*

Gianni. [*shaking his head.*
Always with Antonello!

> *Carlo.* What bring'st thou ?

Barb. [*joyously.*] The sentence is revers'd! Ask Nello, Master.

Ippol. Speak.

    Anton. What she says is true. The Ser Beccari
Is banish'd and his name struck from the rolls,
For plotting against Messere Carlo's life.

Carlo. Ah! [*looking at Angelica, who turning pale presses closer
        to Ippolito. Domicilla and Cornelia evince as-
        tonishment, — Cornelia's not unmingled with
        indignation.*

    Ippol. Speak from the beginning. How is this?

Anton. Ser Giacomo Gradenata — whom I met
One day with little Barba — [*darting a look of sly malice
        at Barbara.*

    Gianni. Ay, I 've seen her
With Ser Beccari too. She 's much too easy,
I 'm thinking, with such fellows: that 's my idea.

Barb. But not affair.

    Angel. Peace, Barba!

    Carlo. And thou, Gianni,
Show more of reverence.

    Ippol. And, good Nello, keep
Thy feuds with Barbara for her private ear.
Thou shalt have full occasion by and by.
Proceed.

    Anton. [*with more of his usual manner, and speaking with
        increasing rapidity as he goes on.*
Ser Giacomo, brib'd by the Beccari,
Made the false charge, but, horrified to find
A murder toward, told all unto his sister.
Monna Camilla goes straightway to the Nine ——

Angel. His sister !

        Ippol. And betroth'd to Gasparo's self!

Barb. [*significantly.*] I think I know the motive.

                    Carlo. Ah! —— The wretch !

Angel. Thou shalt know all a fitter time, Ippolito.

Anton. Yes, Barbara lent her motive to Ser Giac'mo.

Gianni. She lends too many, I 'm thinking, to such gentry.

Ippol. Let Barbara alone, my friends. What then ?

Anton. Both of them banish'd from the State forever —

    Beccari's fortune confiscated — name

    Struck from the rolls —

            Ippol. 'T is retribution just.

Anton. The fine remitted — Messer Montanino

    Restor'd to all his honors.

          Carlo. And thus the weight

    Of seven hundred florins is off my heart.

    Its pulse may now beat freely to thy love,

    Nobie Ippolito.

         Ippol. With thy consent

    I 'll part the seven hundred twixt these three ;

    One half to honest Gianni, and one half

    To Nello and Barba, whom we will make one.

Gianni. [*shaking his head.*

    Best make her one, I 'm thinking, with all mankind.

Barb. Now God forbid, were all like thee !

             Carlo. Peace, girl !

    And thou, old man, rein-in that petulant tongue.

    Fit 't were you us'd it, thou and Barba both,

    In thanking that munificence which makes you

Rich far beyond your sphere.

　　　　　　　Gianni. I am most thankful.

But Messer Carlo, to your father's son
I should not need to boast, who serv'd his sire,
That Gianni, poor and old, takes never money
Save from his master's hand.

　　　　　　　Carlo. Forgive me, Gianni;
Forgive my chiding, — even for those words,
Which show thy tongue takes counsel from thy heart
As well as spleen. [*He extends his hand to Gianni, who
　　　　　　　　　kisses it, with tears.*

　　　　　　　Ippol. Yet take it from my sister,
Who will be soon thy mistress.

　　　　　　　Cornel. And who adds
What she impos'd upon thee at the gate:
For 't is thy due, yet scarcely thy desert; —
For where are honest pride and faith like thine?

Gianni. [*much moved and kissing her hand.*

Madonna, I ne'er thought to live to see
The Montanino and Salimbene join'd,
And cry with joy at it. But I do. I 'm thinking,
Heaven makes some curses blessings; and old times
Have chang'd now for the better; that 's my idea.

ANTONELLO *and* BARBARA *likewise make their acknowl-
edgments to* IPPOLITO, *in dumb show.*

Domicil. Mine, Gianni, too. Yet, dear me! in my day ——
But never mind! I will not change again.

Ippol. Not with the times? Nay, Aunt, play out the play.

Domicil. Don't contradict, Ippol'to dear.   I mean,
    The present happy truce I sha'n't gainsay.
Ippol. Truce ?   'T is a peace : " I 'm thinking," to remain,
    (As Gianni says,) till doomsday.
                    Domicil. And I say,
    Thereto, Amen ! my boy.
               Ippol. Is that the vein ?
    Why then the play is play'd, for good and all.
Cornel. [*in half-whisper.*
    Be it.   Yet, while Aunt Cilla is in train,
    'T were very well to let the Curtain fall.

Curtain falls.

THE MONTANINI

1.—P. 263. THE MONTANINL] The story is founded on the XLIXth Novel of Bandello.

2.—P. 264. CARLO DI TOMMASO MONTANINO.] That is, as subsequently shown (Act I. Sc. 1.), *Carlo son of*, etc. A mode of writing the names of persons that was very common in all parts of Italy in the Middle Ages.

" Olim a Patris nomine, non Senis tantum, sed et in aliis Italiae Civitatibus, consuevere non pauci cognomentum sibi adsciscere. Hinc audias *Piero . di Tegliaccio, Francesco di Messer Vanni, Cione di Vitelluccio, Neri di Guccio,* atque horum similia; hoc est, *Petrum Tegliaccii filium, Francesci Domini Vannis filium,* etc. Rursus in more fuit nomina quaedam contrahere, ac veluti dimidiata adhibere ; nam pro *Alexandro* aliquis appellabatur *Sandro,* pro *Bartholomœo Meo,* pro *Arriguccio,* ut ego arbitror, *Guccio,* pro *Maphœo,* sive *Maffeo, Feo,* pro *Uguccione Cione.* . . . . Infra nobis occurrent *Messer Sozzo Dei,* et *Messer Deo Gucci,* qui alibi appellatur *Messer Deo di Messer Guccio.* Eadem ratione in hisce regionibus nobiles Manfredorum,

Piorum, Picorum, aliorumque familiæ, Patris nomen in suum cognomentum olim verterunt." Murator. *In Chron. Senen. Andr. Dei
præfat. Rer. Ital. Script.* T. **xv.**

3.—P. 264. Salimbeni.] Pronounce the *e* as *a* in *bane.* It is
one of those foreign names which cannot be anglicized without mar-
ring it. So in the name *Bertuccio Arrigucci,* which will occur frequently in the play, sound the first of the two c's as *t* : — *toot'-tcheo,*
— *goot'-tche.*

4.—P. 264. Volpicina.] A character-name, the diminutive of
volpe (she-fox). Pronounce, as in Italian: *Vohl-pe-tche'-nah.*

5.—P. 265. *Ser Gasparo.*] The prefix of courtesy and of reverence, *Sere* or *Ser,* and, in its complete or composite form, *Messere* or
Messer, had at this time been in vogue for only about forty years, if
a note to that effect in Muratori is accepted, and was at first equivalent to *Signore, Signor,* being convertible in the Latin into *Dominus.*
In a later age, *Messere* was confined to members of the bench, doctors,
and priests, as we read in Varchi. Compare note 12 to *Bianca
Capello.*

Muratori, or one of his co-workers, thinks that the word, in the
form *Missere,* came in with the study of the Provensal about the time
of Dante's master, Ser Brunetto Latini. Os. in his vol. above-cited,
in coll. 145, 6, a note to the Sanesan Chronicle of *Neri di Donato.**
Giovanni Villani however applies it to personages in periods long

---

* Still, I do not think that the example adduced by the commentator is con-
clusive, namely, that in a letter of 1265 to one of the Tolomei is written, not
a Messere Tolomeo, but *Domino Tolomeo.* For as *Dominus* was the usual form
in the Latin acts and records, etc., so it was very natural, especially in the mongrel Italian employed in that very writing cited, the words should be interchanged.
See extracts from certain notarial instruments in Notes 1 and 2, p. x. of the *Elogio
di G. V.* T. viii. *Cronica.* ed. cit.

anterior to that epoch, as will be seen presently.* And in fact the reference to Ser Brunetto Latini would itself put its introduction back at least a score of years before the period of 1280 assigned by the Italian archæologist, for Ser Brunetto is named by G. Villani among the Guelfs who fled from Florence to Lucca in 1260 (T. ii. p. 113, *ed. infra cit.*) after the disastrous day of Montaperti. This was five years before the date assigned to the birth of Dante, who addresses his old master by that title in the Shades: "Siete voi qui, *Ser Brunetto ?*" † where it is observable that the plural address of reverence, *voi* for *tu*, is employed.

What the comment on the Sanesan Chronicle advances, that between the word *Messere* and the simple *Sere* the same distinction obtains as was usual with *Madonna* and its contraction *Monna*, — namely, that the briefer term was applied to persons of a relatively inferior condition,‡ as for example, in the case of *Ser*, to notaries and

---

* He goes back indeed as far as the year 1113, under which date, in his 4th Book (c. xxix.), he speaks of "*Messer* Ruberto Tedesco, vicario dello 'mperadore Arrigo in Toscana." It is true, Villani, who was contemporary with Dante, may be supposed to confer the prefix after the fashion of his time.

† Two other instances in Dante illustrate so fully the mode of using both forms as to be in themselves sufficient exemplification. In *Purgatorio* xxiv. we have *Messer* applied to the Cavalier Marchese, and in *Paradiso*, at the close of the xiiith Cto., adopting a name (Martino) to indicate generally any class of illiterate men, he prefixes simple *Ser*, making it correlative with *Donna* (*Monna*, in modern edd.) for the female :

"Non creda donna [monna] Berta e ser Martino."

Here we see *Monna* applied precisely as we do *Madam* and *Mrs*.

‡ "Non si può negare, che nella sua origine *Sere* sia l'istesso che *Signore*; ma è da osservarsi, che i nomi accorciati si davano a persone d'inferior condizione, come è noto ne' titoli di Madonna e Monna. L'uno si dava alle Prencipesse ed anco a quelle Donne di Nobiltà assoluta ; e l'altro alle Donne Nobili, ma non di Condizione Principesca, e alle Donne popolari, ma che erano di Famiglie risedute, restando l'altre senza titolo. . . Così è giustamente avvenuto a' titoli di *Missere* e di *Sere*. Il primo si dava fra gli altri a' Giudici, e Dottori, e l'altro a Notai, che per lo più sono al servigio de' medesimi." *Loc. sup. cit.*

It is indeed a distinction reasonable and natural in itself, that is, arising from

simple priests, to which two classes the annotator would appear to confine it, — is supported by the usage of old writers. In the list of the embassy sent to the Emperor when at Pisa (March 1, 1355), we have the names thus set down: "Misser Guccio di . . . . . Talomei, Giovanni d'Agnolino Salimbeni, Misser Francesco di Misser Bino Giudice de gli Accarigi, Renaldo del Peccio, Davino di Memmo, Giovanni di Tura Neri de' Montanini, Ser Mino di Meo Filippi loro Notajo." *Cron. San.* c. 146. It is at this very passage that the comment I refer to is made, and it certainly of itself sets the matter in a very plain light. The fact too is confirmed by the instance of Brunetto, who was a notary. In the 16th century the distinction continues to be very observable. Thus, while Varchi the historian's father, who was an attorney, is styled simply *Ser* Giovanni, his son is dignified as *Messer* Benedetto, having been endowed by Duke Cosmo with a benefice in Mugello. In that historian's xvth Book (T. v. p. 349 *ed. al. cit.*) we have this noticeable passage, which happily exemplifies both subjects of the note : . . . "un ser Mariotto di ser Luca de' Primi d' Anghiari suo cancelliere " . . where *cancellicre* is evidently used for *segretario*, although in the acceptation of *register of public acts* it would put the person it indicates in the same class with the notary of those days.

But the distinction, though I have thought it of sufficient interest to be noted for the student and the lover of accuracy, is of no consequence, even were it practicable, in a drama in English ; and that I

the customs and thought-habits of men, all contractions in names or titles of address savoring of familiarity, sometimes that of affection or of popularity, or indicating a reverence or respect that is conceded rather than exacted. The *Mrs.* and *Ma'am* of the English, the *Ma'm'selle* (fam. and vulg.) of the French, the *Usted* of the Spanish, are all analogous corruptions ; arising from precisely similar causes, familiarity of intercourse, rapidity of utterance, and the desire to avoid a formality which by its frequent repetition becomes not only stiff but disagreeable. It is probable also that thence, and not, as Webster is inclined to think, from the influence of some Northern language, the word *Master* in compellation took the slender sound of *Mister*.

have disregarded it in the present play, whose action is of 1322, can
scarcely be held a license even by an Italian scholar, especially as
there are authorities who would appear to justify the interchange,*
and even Muratori himself acknowledges, what indeed requires
no demonstration, that *Sere* was originally the same as *Signore*. A
like remark, so far as the unimportance of exactness in these
particulars, in an English play, may be made as to the mode
of placing the prefix, which, in both its forms, is never used
(that I have yet seen) before the name proper, but occurs before
the forename only, precisely as the *Don* (Dominus) of the Spaniard,
and the titular address and designation of a knight or a baronet
in England. †

6.—P. 269. — *the dainty Three . . . my father's day Saw
disinterr'd*, etc.] I have forgotten my authority for this fact. But
the following passage, from a well-written guide-book of travel, ex-
plains fully the text, if it is not indeed the very source to which
perhaps I was indebted.

"In the library [of the Duomo or Cathedral] is also preserved the exquisite
antique group of the Graces in Greek marble, found under the foundations in the
13th century. This group, one of the finest known examples of Grecian sculp-
ture, was copied by Canova, and was so much admired by Raphael that he made

* See in *R. It. Sc.* the note just cited. My disregard however of this distinc
tion, as well as of the mode of employing it, arose probably from the incomplete-
ness of my information at the time. Unimportant as I admit them to be in
English, I should, I think, had I known better, have carefully observed both these
niceties of ancient Italian usage, if only as a point of *costume*. A voluntary error
of the sort would have been a deviation from truth.

† I need hardly add that our *Sir*, used in ordinary compellation, is precisely
the same word. With us too, that is in English, it was anciently given as a title
to priests. It is interesting to observe how in modern intercourse these distinc-
tions become less and less certain and are finally wiped away, precisely as the
plural style of address has almost excluded from ordinary conversation the *thou*
and *thee* which at one time indicated inferiority.

a sketch of it, which is still preserved in the Academy of Venice. It is also supposed to have suggested the picture of the Graces by Raphael, formerly in Sir Thomas Lawrence's collection, and afterwards in that of the late Lord Dudley." BLEWITT's *Handbook of Central Italy*, 2d ed. 1850.

7.—P. 271. *What, my fair Volscian, though not Dian's nymph.*] In allusion to the Camilla of Virgil.

> "Hos super advenit, Volsca de gente, Camilla."
> *Æn.* vii. 803. ed. Hunter: *Andr.* 1799.

> "Est et, Volscorum egregia de gente, Camilla,
> Agmen agens equitum et florentis acre catervas." XI. 433.

Her father had dedicated her when an infant to Diana, in the emergence recounted *ib.* 539, sqq. And the goddess, deploring the fate of the maiden queen, says there:

> "Vellem haud correpta fuisset
> Militia tali, conata lacessere Teucros:
> Cara mihi comitumque foret nunc una mearum."

8.—P. 273. *Thou 'dst like again to venture?*] At this place was inserted in the copy the following stage-direction: *The door above is seen to open a little way, and the face of Camilla appears in the opening.* But in the original Ms., I find I had remarked in the margin: "Or without this; as it is more natural that the door should not be opened, and this indication to the spectators that the party is listening is a commonplace stage-action. Camilla's words at the close of the Scene, and previously the noise she makes behind the door which startles Gaspar, are enough, and more refined, for the printed drama at least."

I am still of that opinion. But for the Stage the by-play, though both unnatural and commonplace, is perhaps requisite, and certainly aids the intelligence of a mixed audience. I shall therefore indicate here, in the Notes, the remaining directions that are omitted from the Scene. They number from this point, 8, to 13 inclusive.

9.—P. 274. *Camilla draws the door to again.*

10.—P. 274. *Giacomo sits again sullenly. Beccari draws his chair closer to him — in so doing looks once more at the door, but it is not yet reopened.*

11.—P. 274. *Camilla appears listening again.*

12.—P. 275. *Camilla, from behind the door, shakes her finger at him.*

13 —P. 275. *Camilla shakes her fist at Giacomo, but in the movement makes a noise, and quickly closes the door, ere Beccari turning hastily can detect her.*

14.—P. 280. *— bowing reverent-low . . . he yields the path,* etc.] The streets of Siena are very narrow; so that the courtesy was almost imperative.

15.—P. 289. *— the Arbia.*] The little stream which flows by Siena.

16.—P. 289. *- the she-wolf —*] The emblem of Siena, which is stuck up in various parts of the city, as the *bear* is in Bern.

17.—P. 289. *— the great Countess —*] Matilda of Tuscany the friend of Pope Hildebrand.

18.—P. 289. *— Sane'si —*] The Italian, or rather, Tuscan name for the people of Siena.

The origin of the city is ascribed by Villani to the old and invalided soldiers of Charles Martel, left by him in that locality in 670; whence its first name *Sena* (and in the pl., for the double strong-

hold, *Senae*), "derivando di quelli che v' erano rimasi per vec-
chiezza " *Cron* I. lvi. p. 73 sq. t. 1, *ed. cit.*

This is contrary to the opinion generally entertained, which would
put it so far back as the *Senensis Colonia* of Pliny. In the Handbook
just cited, we are told : " Siena preserves, almost without change, the
name of Sena Julia, and is supposed to have been a colony established by Julius Cæsar " (meaning probably, in his time).

19.—P. 291. *Gelica* —] This abbreviation of names (here and
elsewhere in the play) was the custom of the day, and is therefore
characteristic of the period of the action. The familiar instance of
the contemporary poet Dante will occur to the reader: *Dante* for
Durante; as the lady he has immortalized by the complete name of
Beatrice was commonly known as *Bice.*

I have touched lightly on this subject before, at p. 256 of this
vol. Comp., above, Notes 2 and 5. In all the modern tongues,
including our own, we are familiar with similar abbreviations. The
difference is, that at the present day the contracted name is often
vulgar, and always familiar, if not disrespectful; in those days it
was of general usage, and conveyed no disparagement, and if not
elegant yet did not savor of vulgarity.

20. – P. 292. *Plotting with Deo of the Tolomei, The banish'd
Guelf!*] He was, with Messer Sozzo Dei, one of the heads of the
conspiracy which had terminated in their expulsion, and that of
their confederates, three years previously. See *G. Villani*, IX.
xcvi. (t. iv. p. 95 *ed. cit.*) The influence of the Salimbeni, who in
part were on the side of the existing government, and the readiness
of the Tolomei, in their feud with that family, to make it an occasion of revolt, are seen in the same chapter. Further on in Book
IX., the mutual enmity, and at the same time the power of these
rival houses, find brief but sufficient illustration in the following
passages: — " Nell' anno 1322, del mese d'Aprile, la città di Siena

fu a romore per cagione che quegli della casa de' Salimbeni uccisono una notte due fratelli carnali figliuoli di cavaliere della casa de' Tolomei, loro nemici, nelle loro case. Per la potenza delle dette due case i Sanesi quasi tutti parati per combattersi insieme, ec." cxlvii. p. 139 sq. "Nel detto anno [1326] . . . il duca di Cala-vra con sua baronia e cavalieri entrò nella città di Siena . . . Trovò la terra molto partita per la guerra ch' era intra 'Tolomei e' Salimbeni, che quasi tutti i cittadini chi tenea coll' uno e chi coll' altro . . . e 'l duca così fece, che tra le due case Tolomei e Salimbeni fece fare triegua con sofficiente sicurtà cinque anui" . . . ccclvi. p. 343 sq.

In 1337, they made peace together at the command of the Pope. *Cron. San.* R. I. S. xv. 96.

21.—P. 292. *Condemn'd to pay*, etc.] This was a constant mode of punishment, presumably for the rich and powerful. Thus, in the year of our play, fifteen of the Tolomei were mulcted, three of them in a thousand florins each. *Cron. San.* u. c. 54.

22.—P. 297. — *who could lend the State*, etc.] "Incontanente si provvidono [i Sanesi e gli usciti ghibellini] di moneta, e accattaro dalla compagnia de' Salimbeni, che allora erano mercatanti, ventimila fiorini d'oro, e puosono loro pegno la rocca a Tentennana, e più altre castella del comune." *G. Vill.* VI. lxxvi. (*ed. cit.* II. p. 104.) *Cs.* Note 24.

23.—P. 309. *The people do not like you any more Than do the nobles*; etc.]

"Era per lunghi tempi governato il reggimento della Città di Siena per l'ordine di Nove, il quale era ristretto in meno di novanta Cittadini, sotto certo industrioso inganno: però che quando il tempo veniva di fare i loro generali squittini, acciò che ogni degno cittadino popolare entrasse nello ordine de' Nove, coloro che haveano già usurpati gli Uficj si ragunavano segretamente in una Chiesa, e

17*

ivi disponeano di alcuni cui e' voleano che rimanessono nell' ordine, fermandoli tra loro per saramento. E prometteano tutti dare
a' detti le loro boci co' lupini neri, e tutti gli altri, che andavano
allo squittino, ch' erano molti buoni e degni Cittadini, gli riprovavano
co' lupini bianchi, si che l'ordine non crescea più che volessono : nè
alcuno v'entrava che tra loro in prima non fosse diliberato : Per la
qual cosa erano in odio a tutti gli altri popolani, e a grande parte
de' nobili, con cui non s'intendeano. Eranvi certi, che manteneano
questa città, e guidavano il comune, come e' voleano." M. VILLANI.
IV. c. lxi. in *Rer. Ital. Script.* XIV. coll. 278 sq. The historian
goes on to show, how, with the desire to debase and disfranchise
Florence by the power of Charles IV., the chiefs in the government
of the Nine made over their own liberties to that Emperor.

24.—P. 314. — *their enormous wealth* —] A note to the Sanesan
Chronicle (*l. c.* coll. 96, 7) attests at once the great wealth and the
large commerce of this powerful family. For their wealth, it will be
sufficient to quote the first paragraph. "In quest' anno 1337 si osserva
la gran ricchezza de' Salimbeni. Qui si legge : 'Benuccio di Giovanni
Salimbeni era in questo. tempo 1337. Camarlengo, e distribuitore
de le Casate de' Salimbeni Nobili di Siena, cioè de' censi, e argentiera,
e ramiera, donde che più anni avea a distribuire infra 16. capifa-
miglie di Salimbeni circa a fiorini cento mila d'oro." For their commerce, it is said that they sold in the single month of January of the
succeeding year (1338) "ottanta borse ["borse da spose d'oro,"
elsewhere] per 80. spose novelle di Casate de' Nobili di Siena "
Whereupon the commentator adds the remark, " that it demonstrates
sufficiently the great riches the Sanesan people made by traffic, as it
further makes evident the great Nobility that was then in Siena,
he not supposing it possible that in any city whatever of Italy in
his own time there could in a single year be made eighty marriages
among families actually noble."

25.—P. 325. — *and when the Nine Begin to totter*, etc.] It was not till thirty-three years afterward that the iniquitous government was put down by Charles IV., in violation of his own engagement. See *Matt. Villani;* who remarks philosophically: " E pare degna cosa, che coloro, i quali ingannano in Comune i loro Cittadini, e rompono la fede a' loro amici, che alcuna volta per quella medesima sieno puniti, e portino pena de' peccati commessi." *ad init. cap.* lxxxi. col. 294. The Emperor entered Siena the 25th of March, 1355, whereupon the Tolomei, Malavolti, Piccolomini, Saracini, and those of the Salimbeni who were opposed to the corrupt magistracy, with a concourse of common people, raised the cry of "Viva lo 'mperadore, e muojono i Nove e le gabelle ! " There occurred the usual scenes of violence, with death to some, and spoliation ; the expulsion of the Nine and their families. The next day the Emperor forbad forever the office and order. All who had taken part in the Government, to escape the danger and the infamy with which they were regarded as traitors to their own country, went into foreign lands. *ib.* lxxxii. col. 295. The Chronicle of Neri di Donato records the event with more force and greater detail. The Emperor swears to preserve the order of the Nine. (They had sent an embassy to him. See note 5, above, also note 23 *ad c.*, p. 394.) He enters, *the 23d* of March, to the cry of " Viva Lomperadore, e muoja li Nove ! " cuts the chains of the city the 24th. The next day, the 25th, Siena in arms. Charles revokes his oath and annuls all the privileges conceded. — The account of the riot, and its violence, and the overthrow of the Nine, is very full in this chronicler. Robbery ; arson ; death and wounds to some of the order, complete ruin to all, whom none, not even the clergy, would succor. *Ad ann.* 1355.

26.—P. 332. — *five hundred golden Johns !*] On one side of the florin of gold was the image of John the Baptist, with the legend 'Santo Giovanni Battista "; on the other the lily of the republic (whence its name), with " Fiorenza."

It was in 1252, in a period of great prosperity and elation, after victories over their rivals, that the Florentines commenced the coining of this famous piece, gold money not being then in use with them. As it was of extraordinary fineness, it came at once into great repute, and its value was so jealously regarded that for nearly 300 years we find scarcely any if any change either in the weight or the quality of the metal.* Villani tells us the florins were twenty-four carats fine and that eight of them weighed an ounce (*Cron.* VI. liii.); Varchi, a little more than twenty-three and seven-eighths in fineness (*St. Fior.* t. v. p. 61. *ed. al. cit.*), and that every hundred weighed an exact pound (t. iii. p. 115). But as the latter is so particular in his statement, it may be that he has only expressed with precision what Villani described in general terms.

The florin of gold was also called a ducat (V. *ib.* III. 117), as here in Act IV. Sc. 2, and throughout *Bianca.*

Of course, while the nominal value was the same, as estimated in *lire* and *soldi*, the actual worth of the coin varied in different ages (see *Varchi* as above, III. 117, 118), and at that distant day a thousand florins of gold, though in computation but little more than so many of our gold dollars, was a very considerable sum of money.

27.—P. 345. *Messer Provenzano*, etc.] At *Colle di Valdelsa*, in 1269, when the Florentine Guelfs defeated the Ghibellines of Siena and their allies of the same faction, and avenged the disaster of Montaperti. "Il Conte Guido Novello si fuggì, e messere Provenzano Salvani signore e guidatore dell' oste de' Sanesi fu preso, e tagliatoli il capo, e per tutto il campo portato fitto in su una lancia. E bene s' adempiè la profezia e revelazione che gli avea fatta il diavolo per via d'incautesimo, ma non la intese; che avendolo fatto constrignere per sapere come capiterebbe in quella oste, mendacemente

* This had its natural consequence. They not only rose in value in 1531, but they were withdrawn from circulation, and melted or hoarded. VARCHI, *ut s.* III., 117, sq. & V. 61.

rispuose, e disse: anderai e combatterai, vincerai no morrai alla bat-
taglia, e la tua testa fia la più alta del campo; e egli credendo avere
la vittoria per quelle parole, e credeudo rimanere signore sopra tutti,
non fece il punto alla fallacie, ove disse: vincerai no, morrai ec. E
però è grande follia a credere a sì fatto consiglio come quello del
diavolo" G. VILLANI. VII. xxxi. (T. II. p. 195.)

28.—P. 347. *Fit to live.* Giac. *Camilla! — Woman! — Stop!*]
This is quite equal in time to the ten-syllable Iambic, — the emphasis in the three last words of the preceding verse being on "art."
The regular measure however may be observed, by simply substitu-
ting "Worthy" for "Fit," and putting the emphasis on "not." But
the passage loses thereby strength and propriety. "Fit" is the
word *Camilla* would have used.

THE SCHOOL FOR CRITICS.

It is not my fault that this comedy is written. I should willingly have been at peace even with the small pretenders who prototype its characters; but they would not let me. All the personal consequences of its publication must rest with me alone. My bookseller has in it no interest but that of a commission-merchant, — which is less than some of its famous persons enjoy in the abortion and assignation advertisements of their daily issue.

L. O.

321 West Nineteenth-Street.
January 26, 1868.

THE SCHOOL FOR CRITICS

OR

A NATURAL TRANSFORMATION

MDCCCLXVII — VIII

CHARACTERS

Sus Minervam, *A.M., LL.D.; Editor of the* Ethnical Quarterly Review.

Anicula, *Editress, under Bodkin, of the* Ethnos.

Fledgling, *Literary Critic, under Flunky Weathercock, of the* Hotchpot Hours.

Deadhead, *Literary Critic, under Polyphemus, of the* Hotchpot Cryer.

Heartandhead, *a retired Author and Critic.*

Atticus, *Literary Reader for the* Brookbank Publishing-house.

Galantuom, *Literary Critic of the* Hotchpot Civis.

Saltpeter,
Brimstone, } *Underground gentlemen, on a mundane excursion.*
Charcoal,

Scene. *Slanghouse-Square and its neighborhood, in Hotchpot City.*

Time. *That occupied by the action.*

THE SCHOOL FOR CRITICS

SCENE. *A street, at its opening into Slanghouse-Square.*

Enter

BRIMSTONE, SALTPETER *and* CHARCOAL, *encountering.*

Brim. Well, old Salt (since our Hell-coin'd names,
  Nor our Heaven-stamp'd either, can here be given),
  Missest thou not those jolly blue flames,
  Which, though — not quite as soft
  As the smokeless rays aloft
  In the region men call Heaven —
  They kept us mostly waking
  With a something like heart-aching,
  And never promis'd slaking
  Like the one day Earth's hell claims

For a solace out of seven,
Yet were bliss supreme, I swear,
To the weariness we are driven
To encounter in this air ?

Salt. The weariness ! disgust.
Why, Brim, thou 'rt losing fire.
Man's treachery, his lust,
His ferocity —— What boots
Comparing them with brutes ?
These things wake mirth, not ire.
The trait which stirs my spleen
Is to find the beast so mean.

Brim. But then own it, as is just,
All Hell holds no such liar.

Char. That is because we have no Press.
Although we dabble so largely in steam,
We cannot throw off ream by ream
Of lies and nonsense, I must confess.
'T is an institution that should be ours.
Its sire was help'd by the Devil they say.
I saw on the wall of a house one day
A picture announcing a new old play.
A printing-press stood in the sky,
Held up by a cloud, while on a floor,
In a redtail'd coat which he never yet wore,
Stood who do you think old Faust before,
And pointed to the machine on high ;
Who but the chief of the Infernal Powers ?

Salt. Had the thing been stuck in a hole below,

It had show'd too plainly its use you know,—
As they use it here in Slanghouse-Square.[1]

Char. What name is that?

          Salt. One of apery,
In all humility stolen, I hear,
By the loose-hing'd Weathercock quivering here,
From his ponderous model across the sea.
In front is the palace in rogues abounding,
Who draw from the public pot their fare,
And openly and at all times dare
What to us is perfectly astounding,
Who scent more filth in this upper air
Than would cover all Hell and leave to spare
Out of its fathomless superabounding.[2]

    On that right-hand corner, half sharp, half flat,
With perpetual simper and old white hat,
The rider of hobbies plies his trade,
Who thinks the rest of mankind were made,
At least that are male,
To be led by the nose and follow his tail.
Ambitious and hankering for display,
But not so genteel
By a very great deal
As Flunky Weathercock over the way,
He joy'd to become an arch-traitor's bail,
And journey'd far
To the Southern star
To take the seraphical man by the hand
Who fill'd with ashes and blood this land.

Char. I understand.

'T was an offer for station.

Brim. A bid for the votes of the Southern nation,
When they come again to have command.
He wanted to cut the Union in two,
And would do it in four,
If so it would give him three chances more
To set his white head white and black heads o'er, —
Which is what the Weathercock would not do.

Salt. They are going to make an envoy, they say,
Of Flunky.

      Brim. Aha! That is why, one day,
To get appointed,
To the People's Anointed
He veer'd, then the next, to be confirm'd,
To the People's deputies daintily squirm'd,
And turn'd his tail the other way ?[3]

Salt. But let him alone, he is not our game.
He is mean enough, like his fellows around,
To put, if unseen, his nose in the ground,
But sets too much store by an honest name
(That bauble, you wot, human knaves have found
To dazzle fools and their wits confound)
To eat dry sawdust and swallow flame.
Behind you, — turn round, —
There is Bodkin's *Ethnos*, that olio sheet
Where stale pretension and jargon meet,
Affected science, dogmatic cant,
And ignorance glaz'd by amusing rant,

And what to us three makes its charm complete,
An air of candor, high-pitch'd yet sweet,
Which Sus Minervam himself can't beat.
'T is there we are bound.

Char. For what?

     Salt. Thou shalt see.

If the little old woman, whose girls there prepare
The dirty linen for public wear,
Should prove short-handed and pitch on me,
Why then Sus Minervam, A.M., LL.D.,
May add three points to his double degree.
Come, Charcoal, Brim, let us onward fare.

Brim. But give us to know of this mystery.

Char. And what our Master may want of us three.

Salt. So 't is something to do,
 What recks it? You two
 Are weary like me of this sluggish air.
 But this much is given
 Ye both to know:
 There is a fellow who wrote of Heaven
 And human wo
 And all that stuff of the Cross you know,
 Who has ventur'd a dip in the lake below
 And fish'd us up, to give us brains.

Brim. What an impudent gift!

     Salt. More than ye think.

 To make us ramble like men in drink,
 With fustian phrases and sense obscure,
 Would picture us falsely, to be sure,

But would be worth the pains:
For fustian maintains our name's illusion
With man who is dazzled by word-confusion,
And finds magnificent and grand
All that his noddle can't understand,
And weighty the thoughts from whose tangled skeins
He fails to draw a conclusion.
Sus and Anicula, Fledgling too,
Though, like his master, he points both ways,
Help us a great deal nowadays
By keeping this great point in view, —
Save when his hireling pencil strays
From the false and absurd to what is true.

Char. So lucid Longfellow got his due.

Brim. Not when he labor'd to give to view
The fanciful picture the Tuscan drew
Of a place that is known to me and you.

Salt. Ay, Fledgling was then in his element,
Serving the Devil with double intent:
To lick up with neatness
The spittle of greatness,
And parade his own mock sentiment.
Thus the uncouth phrase and the limping line
Were held out to asses as grain divine,
And stirring up rubbish he cry'd, "Oh fine!"

Brim. What would ye have?   Was not Swinburne's stuff,
And Ruskin's and Emerson's affectation,
And Carlyle's Dutch made bright enough
To Fledgling's ratiocination?

Though the general mass of the reading nation,
Beating the thicket for explanation,
Might sooner guess at futurity,
Seeing we, who are us'd to what is tough
And the brightness that makes obscurity
In our underground relation,
Were wrapt in amaze
By the multiple blaze,
And lost our calculation.

Salt. Why you 've grown quite letter'd, old fellow Brim,
Since in coat and breeches here sojourning!

Brim. 'T is part of my universal knowledge.
I have the insight
By infernal right,
As Sus got his at College.
I am not indeed A.M. like him,
Nor mean to purchase the other degree,
But I have an equal facility
In affecting all kinds of learning.
I think, had I a pen in hand,
And a cylinder press at my command,
Like Flunky, Brooks and Greeley,
I might do a devilish deal of good,
Like them, or the *World*, or Benjamin Wood,
Though I cannot lie so freely.

Salt. You shall do something better, and teach these fools,
Especially Sus, and Bodkin's piddler,
A lesson yet new in the Critics' schools,
That they who dance must pay the fiddler.

Char. Old fellow, well said:

One would think you were bred

An apprentice here in Slanghouse-Square.

Salt. 'T is the cruelest thing you could have said.

I thought we devils had still some head,

Despite of our brimstone air.

But enough.   Let us move.   Ere the sun be gone

To the West with his clouded nightcap on,

Ye shall both of you see,

And luminously,

Into the pool of this mystery

Whose bottom is visible only to me,

And shall help me a comedy prepare.

Char. Amen! as said on his knees Jeff Davis,

When he pray'd "From our enemies, O Lord, save us,

And let them be damn'd!"•   So mote it be!

I scent in the night-air a jolly spree.

Brim. Pitch and naphtha!   (I hate to swear —

But Milton taught me.)   'T will set us free

From the chain of this damnable earth-ennui.

Char. And for the rest may the Devil care. [*Exeunt Diab.*

Enter
DEADHEAD *and* FLEDGLING.

Fledg. Well met, *Caput Mort.:* though our masters agree,

Like two pickpockets, to scold each other,

That is meant to blind the world, but binds not you and me.

To us the phrase applies,

Crows pluck not out crows' eyes;

And we servants of the lamp,

Though we call each other scamp,

Yet, like beggars on a tramp,

Are each to the other hail-fellow and a brother.

Dead. Ay, 't is nuts to see the crowd,

Because we scold aloud,

Think both of us too proud

To shake each other's paw and swig hobnob together;

But, let it rain, old fellow,

They 'll find the same umbrella

Protects your stovepipe hat and my old felt from the

weather.

Fledg. Why, bravo! you improve:

That 's a figure now I love.

Don't be angry if I put it in my *Minor Notes* to-morrow.

Though, believe, I scorn to steal,

Save when hard-up for a meal,

Yet no one can object that now and then I borrow.

Dead. Very well; I 'll take my turn.

Fledg. Agreed. But I say, Dead, —

Ah, you know not how I yearn

To ask you on this head! —

Has your scribeship haply redd

The drama on the Cross

And those others ——

                    Dead. — To our loss

Which some upstart bard ——

                    Fledg. You err;

'T is an old hand at the game;
That is plain.   Besides, his name
Fits the collar of the cur
That snarl'd at us before
For the blackguard stuff we wore
And the lies we daily swore
In the Press.
As playwrights both ourselves,
Who have had our trash by twelves
Laid on the playhouse shelves,
'T is to Number One we owe it,
That our scorner, this d——d poet,
Lack success.
Have you redd him?

    Dead. 'Faith, not I.

Does it need to read, to damn?
Besides, old 'coon, I am,
Like yourself, prodigious shy
Of all writings where the style
Is above the common run,
Or where wit excludes low fun,
Nor the author has begun
To make it worth my while.

Fledg. I like your humor, but not your facts;
 You hint too plainly at certain acts
 Which we never commit in the *Hotchpot Hours*

Dead. The devil you don't!   Now, by the Powers,
 That is too cool.
 Do you take me, Fledgy, to be a fool?

Know not all men, do not all men see,
We differ in form, not in kind nor degree?
For scandalous tales of vice and fraud,
And quack advertisements that serve the bawd,
And abortionists' invitations,
For all that debauches both soul and mind,
You are not an inch from us behind
And our counters might change stations.
Nay your Sunday sheet, which you loudly swore
Was the people to serve and would end with the war,
Peddles tales, as it spouted bombs before,
And is one of our institutions.
I should like to know what this all is for,
If it is not done to get you more
Of four-penny contributions?
You know we are both rogues in fine ——

Fledg. In the world's sense, Heady, but not in mine,
Who hold that safety and honor bid, —
Here both combine, —
That we should of this high-topt fellow get rid,
Whose old-time light, that will not be hid,
Will clap on our bushel an extra lid,
And make it more hard to dine.
So be cautious, my jewel.

Dead. Be not afraid.
For all some folk in the woods may deem us,
We never do nothing unless we are paid,
Me and my governor, Polyphemus.

Fledg. You 're right, by Jove. Had the cash been tipt,

I don't think any such flam had slipt

As those into which Bodkin's quarto dipt. —

Dead. No, none of us are so squeamous.[6]

Fledg. You are right, old boy, though your grammar is **wrong.**

But I 'm not much us'd to grammar myself.

The whole of Murray 's not worth a song.

It hampers genius; to get along,

All that we need is the love of pelf.

But let us be cautious, and keep to our tracks,

For our pride's defence ——

　　　　　　Dead. And the Revenue Tax.

You see I am sprightly and well may meddle

With playing my governor's second fiddle.

Are you off for your post? I am bound to mine,

Where opposite sandstone our marbles shine.

Fledg. Well, remember to give that fellow a line.

Dead. Be sure, if — you know — inspiration lacks.

Fledg. You need not read him: I sha'n't myself —

Save a page to seem knowing. Misrepresentation

Of authors, though blinding the innocent nation,

Lays never their critics on the shelf.

You know we stab behind their backs.

Our scraps will die, and ourselves unknown

Can indulge our malice and not be known :

None asks if a David have hurl'd the stone,

Or a ragamuffin beggar.

If the world but knew

It was I and you,

We should hardly dare say what we do,

And our pottage would prove *soupe maigre.*

It is such a delight,

To perch on a stool,

And write dunce and fool,

Under the shade of the veil'd gas-light,

And know on the morrow

The author in ire, or it may be in sorrow

If the creature is poor,

Has a sickly wife and a starving child,

Will find himself by a stroke of the pen ——

Dead. A stab in the back.

       Fledg. Ay, — for ever exil'd

From the coveted Eden of famous men,

And, door by door,

Seek in vain for a publisher evermore!

Is n't that to be mighty? It adds, my dear,

Breadth to our breast and a bead to our beer.

Dead. Let us have some, Fledgy.

       Fledg. You soul, I am here.

    Exeunt affectionately together.

ACT THE SECOND

SCENE. *Anicula's Sanctum.*

Enter SUS MINERVAM.

Sus. Out?   What a pity!   It is more than a pity.
What shall I do?   This monstrous Hotchpot City,
Too small a cradle for my pregnant fame,
Will frown indignant on my letter'd name,
If I, who am its snuff, its salt, its scalpingknife and cautery,
Lack pepper for this pupping quarter's Quarterly.
The case is bad, and there is no evasion.
She comes!   I will address her grandly,
That she may listen to me blandly
And minister unto my great occasion.

Enter ANICULA.

Thou stay and glory of Bodkin's Press,
From its primal T to its ultimate letter,
O render me help in my sore distress,
And I'll be forever your debtor!
O et præsid'ium et dulcè decus' meum',
Have you no more "rejected", to give me some?
Shake up your old drawers, and find me a few

To swell out my Quarterly Review;
Oh do!

Anic. Plague on you, Sus! can't you scribble, yourself?
I sold you the last rubbish on my shelf.
There was the scandal of the Piedmont poet,
With its pretended knowledge and false taste,
And its translations, which, not done in haste,
Yet were so vapid that they seem'd to show it.
. And there was the fustian stuff on Rowley,
Who is made to declaim so rantipolly,
While his critic agape cries " Grand! Sublime!"

Sus. Stop there, old angel. 'T was not my crime.
Little vers'd as I am in nature or art,
I saw both were outrag'd, from the start.
Amus'd at once, and not less astounded,
I fear'd all Hotchpot would be confounded,
At the time.
Have pity, that 's a dear good soully!
I am in such a muss,
And have shaken the dust from my wit-bag wholly.

Anic. Don't bother me, Sus.
My girls are at work, and 't is all they can do
To make shifts for me, let alone for you.
But I know of a means: it is *entre nous.*

Sus. Sure; I 'll take ten times my oath.

Anic. As you will not keep it, one time will do.
There is an odd fellow will serve us both.
He was here but now, will be here again. —

Sus. O my delight!
    18*

Anic. Old boy, be quiet!
Would you rob my virtue?

          Sus. No, to be plain,
There is none of it left.

         Anic. You beast, I deny it.
I have lent it at times to you and to others,
Stock-gamesters and politicians bold,
But 't is as immaculate as my old mother's
The day I was foal'd.

Sus. Well?

    Anic. But hands off! This fellow, who is
A queer sort of devil and much of a quiz,
Works quickly and cheaply.

         Sus. Cheaply? O joy!
He may aid me for nothing!

         Anic. Very likely, my boy.
You are not very nice,
In phrases or sense,
(Which lessens the price,)
And if you dispense
With fixing the theme ——

         Sus. Let him scrawl what he will,
So I have not to pay and the scribble will sell.

Anic. In fact, he charg'd nothing for mine. 'T was a favor.
So I let him select. There 's a tragical shaver
Whom he wanted to crush, for making Hell logical,
For giving man's passions to Judas Iscariot,
For not putting Christ in a fiery chariot,
And, with syntax and prosody,

Which ought not in the Cross to be,
Bowing respect to laws etymological.

Sus. Heh! heh! that is funny!
A similar jumble came posted to me.
And as the confector requested no money ——

Anic. Confectioner.

    Sus. No. 'T is confector I mean.
I us'd the phrase learnedly, wittily too,
With a double-entendre quite fresh, smart, and clean,
As, in one of its senses, your *Webster* will show. —

Anic. But you spoke of a jumble.

    Sus. And it was one, I trow,
A jumble, old woman, to you and to me.
As the mixer was flippant enough to seem airy,
I stitched him with Rowley and Victor Alfieri,
In my last Quarterly, — which see.
It is there as it reach'd me, and in no wise doth vary
Except in the learning which fits LL.D.

Anic. 'T was the same fingers doubtless that jumbled for me.
Mine was sheer lies from beginning to end.

Sus. And mine. Greater nonsense there could not well be.
Not even boy Chatterton's trumpery
Was worse. But still 't was the Devil's god-send,
That nondescript mishmash on *Calvary.* .

Anic. Mum! Fledgling comes. Don't be tempted to brag
Of our gratis co-worker. Do as you see me.

Sus. I will do as befitteth my double degree,
Rest assur'd, ma'am, nor let the cat out of the bag.

Enter FLEDGLING.

Anic. Good day, Fledgling Minor.

      Fledg. Old dame, how do' do ?

 You have done a fine thing. Sus Minerv', how are you ?

 I thought to praise one, and I find two instead.

 But as your duality,

 In this critical matter

 Whereof I would chatter,

 Presents but a unity in its reality,

 You are both so alike

 In what both have said

 (Believe not I flatter ;

 Any fool it would strike

 As well as myself in my strong ideality),

 You have lost, sir and ma'am, each the nice speciality'

 Of individuality,

 And, a great generality,

 I may group the totality

 Of my *pensées* on both on this point 'neath one head.

Anic. Little Fledgy, you 're learning,

 I see, in your yearning,

 Your proud spirit burning

 And claws of earth spurning,

 Your small wings to spread.

 You 've consulted Ralph-Waldo, I opine, on that head.

 Excuse me for going. As Sus and I

 Are to be in your panegyric blended.

 What is aim'd at him, if for both intended,

Will hit me too in the very eye.

You have left I see your Minor key

And are strumming it largely on Major-C.

But pray don't take either of us for a flat,

While playing your sharps.   Sus, remember the cat.

[Exit.

Fledg. What does the harridan mean by that?

Sus. I vow'd not to tell.

But as in the *Hours* — 't was on Sunday, 't is true;

That is Flunky's venality, comes not of you —

But as in the *Hours* you quoted me freely,

Much more so than Greeley,

And so made me sell,

I will tell you in confidence;

But do, pray, be on your fence,

And not the fact spill.

Fledg. To one only, — Deadhead.

          Sus. Him only then. —   Well,

What is the stuff which we write so alike upon?

Fledg. " Virginia " and " Calvary."

Sus. Homer, and Dante —— No, the Devil —— You see,

There 's an odd sort of fellow we both chanc'd to strike
    upon,

Who made the same nonsense for both him and me.

But I improv'd mine, as behoov'd my degree,

And made my points good

•By Fernando Wood,

As evidence of my Latinity.

Fledg. Made your points good!   Unmade them, you mean.

Why even Fernando would beat you there clean,
Or, as Dante's great double would say, " *dead* beat."
What a phrase is that![8] —   If you want to lie
Against an author, you should not quote,
My little old fellow, but do as did I
In my Minor Note, —
For his language I knew would reveal the cheat.

Sus. Don't call me old; for I 'm yet in my prime.
I am perhaps little, but oh! sublime.
What I said then of Homer and Virgil and Dante
Proves my knowledge and genius, albeit 't was scanty.

Fledg. It had better been out though, or laid on the shelf
For another occasion, for on my blind soul,
Though I don't know much of those Grecians myself,
As my time is not given to study but pelf,
There was nothing of fitness or sense in the whole.
The exordium of an epic tale
And the opening scene of a tragedy,
Although, like the multiple flimsy thread
The spider passes from out her tail,
They may both be spun from a single head,
Are not the same web any dunce may see,
Nor was there the least conciunity
In all the rest you said.

Sus. Why do you prate thus unto me?
Am I not an LL.D.?
And A.M. too, as it is express'd?
A fledgling — not of your family,
But of that lofty scholastic nest,

Which in all countries, as late I said,
And in all ages, — before there were
Or scholars or schools, you may infer,
Where fools are taught to scribble for bread, —[9]
On its annual brood is made to confer ——

Fledg. Gratis?

      Sus. O no! that were to err —
Those letters which at our tails attest
We are ting'd of the color of the dead.

Fledg. But that must be hard?

          Sus. Hard! Look at me.
See how I flourish my double degree.
There is nothing I give to the world, my dear,
But there my tailpieces both appear,
To signify my brains are Sear;
Yet I am not paler, as you may see,
Than if I belong'd not to the blest.
In Heidelberg, so runs the tale,
Where they keep these tickle-me-ups for sale,
A British noble got LL.D.
Conferr'd on his horse.[10]

        Fledg. You joke.

          Sus. 'T is true.

Fledg. Why not his ass?

      Sus. Had he so thought best.
And why not as well as for you or me?
A letter'd ass — " haud absurdum est."
'T is " *facere* well reipublicæ." [11]

Fledg. What 's all that gibberish?

             Sus. Learned words

I wear at top, like Panza's curds,

To keep my brainpan soft and warm.

They have no meaning, but do no harm,

And help my LL.D. A.M.

Whenever I sport that double degree, —

Which is four times a year; and you must admit

There is not an ass it would better fit,

I bray so mellifluously.

But that is self-praise.   But, you made me warm.

Fledg. Excuse, old fellow : I meant no harm.

   Here, shake our fist.

There is one thing, however, we all forget :

This bard, they say, is a satirist,

And may turn the tables on us yet.

Though I fear not, I ;

For Duyckinck, on whom we may rely, —

His book is a great one — bigger by half

Than Webster's, or the Bible ;

Some of the copies are bound in calf! ——

Sus.   A feature perhaps to make one laugh,

Who knows that its censure is mostly chaff

And its praises are a libel.

Fledg. It may be so.   I never read

Such gallimaufries, not I indeed ;

I should grope there in vain for fruit or seed

To stock my garden of *Minors.*

But Duyckinck says, he had no success.

His *Vision* "fell stillborn from the press ; "

Perhaps because he lack'd cleverness,
Not to shine, but to use the shiners.

Sus. Then Duyckinck says what is not true,
And what *could* not be such he very well knew,
As is patent to me, though not to you
Who were yet in the nest. But the fact is this:
The hairy babe was a bouncing boy,
And crow'd and laugh'd to his daddy's joy,
And to the heirless neighbors' annoy,
Who envied him his bliss.
But he found ere long its nurses were cheats:
They took their wages, but spar'd their teats,
To feed their own brood which did not pay.
So the father took the child away.

Fledg. In plainer words?

     Sus. He stopp'd the sale,
By cutting off the book's supply:
A fact he himself took care to imply
At a somewhat later day.
Such books as that do not often fail.
It is true, neither you nor I was then
In the trade which puts down rising men,
Although there was then black-mail.
You may judge though Duyckinck's malignity,
From the misspell'd name at the article's top
To the close where he calls him a travel'd fop,
And has the astounding audacity,
For a work like that, and from such as he,
To deny him, except as an oddity,

A niche in his hall of letters.
I know not what other men may think, —
Some find sweet odors in things that stink, —
But it would not be with his betters.

Fledg. Hi! hi! do you laud him thus? yet choose
To scribble him down?

                        Sus. Not more I deem
Than others in heart have done and do
Who find a pleasure like curs, it would seem,
In lifting the leg at a profitless muse,
While they yelp as a publisher's puffer;
Than *Ethnos*, the long *Round Robin*, and you,
And your ape across the Eastern stream,
The *Wart-City Buzzard's* stuffer.
However, the fellow should be content,
If he is only a curious ornament
To which Heaven has nothing substantial lent,
As with Milton, or even with Beattie,
That the Barnum of letters has spar'd him a nook
In the rummage-drawer showshop for general look,
His two-volume Cyclopedei'acal book
Of American literati.

Fledg. So, so; that is frank.   And yet yet you admit
Against him what neither has sense nor wit!
Was it done in a Duyckinckish splenetic fit,
Or is it your love to scoff?

Sus. For an ass, you have got in the highway for once.
Like you, I love to call "Dull!" and "Dunce!"
It makes one seem sensible for the nonce.

Then, I hop'd he would buy me off.

Fledg. You try'd that game against the College.
But Præses your hints would not even acknowledge,
And sneer'd both Freshman and Soph. —
But why did you not, for deception's sake,
Between your nonsense a difference make
And the stuff in Bodkin's quarto?
The faults in grammar and English alone,
Without the falsehoods and impudent tone
And puerile pertness, would any one strike
As drawn from one ditch: in fact, they are like
As Port is to Oporto.

Sus. What matters it? The world may say
What it likes; it may call you Beaumarchais;
Me Pindar, or Greeley Cupid:
'T is known I buy up all hackney'd and tame
Rejected articles. Where is the blame?
They 're the only stuff for which I pay,
At least in the literary way,
And I 'ld swear the *Ethnos* does the same,
Though it never was else than stupid.

Fledg. In one thing, though, you may claim to be
More than its match.
                              Sus. In hypocrisy?
Why yes, in that, and post-mortem scandal,
No prick-fame can hold to me a candle.
The Round-Robin try'd it on *Calvary,*
Which he damn'd with a slaver of sympathy,
And smil'd like a king benignant:

But 't is Bowery-acting to my pretence
Of friendliness and benevolence,
Where impertinent and malignant.
You try'd it in the post-mortem line,   •
And fancy'd you'd done it egregiously fine,
When out of your press issu'd Byron a swine;
But look how I Circe'd Alfieri !

Fledg. 'T was done in my finest retributive mood,
Because Alger, in his *Solitude,*
Had blown him upward as extra good,
A kind of Castalian fairy.[12]

Sus. Eh ! I thought you lik'd such soap-bubble stuff.

Fledg. When not too frothy, and *quantum suff.*

Sus. 'T is your Swinburne over again in prose,
But a little more liquid, with more repose,
And Emerson's verse without rhyming close
And a devilish deal less tough.[13]

Fledg. What then? we must worship such men, while yet
Their fame is up and their life not set :
In secret thinking, I go as you go,
And hold Ralph-Waldo, albeit my pet,
As pompous an ass as Victor Hugo,
Who seems to think it his right divine
To bray for all others asinine,
And, hating the right divine of kings,
Is in his pride and his ostentation,
His spirit of logical domination,
Elation and affectation,
The very tyrant he prates of and sings.[14]

Sus. Eu'ye! that 's truth without dilution.

    I cannot see how it got into your sconce.

    After that mouthful, my Minorite dunce, '

    You may lie for a month and have absolution.

Fledg. But don't let out that it was my say :

    Such notions would ruin my trade at once.

    Here hobbles Anicula this way.

    I am off. It is more than I can do,

    To parry and thrust both with her and with you.

Enter ANICULA.

    Good day, old lady ; I 'll in by and by,

    When no one can come 'twixt your beauties and I.

Anic. And me.

        Fledg. Never mind. You might pass the bad grammar,

    For the soft soap it carries. [*Aside.*] The impertinent!

        d—n her !

    'Bye, Sus Minervam, A.M., LL.D.

    The greatest critic that ever could be

    Would be one to unite

    The crepuscular glow of your learning's rushlight

    With Anicula's sterling vacuity. [*Exit.*

Enter SALTPETER.

Anic. He has vanish'd in time, the magpie and ape. —

    Here enters a beast of another shape,

    And bird of another feather.

'T is the gentleman who,

I mentioned to you,

Would do for us both together.

Let me make you acquainted.

This short sturdy man, who looks like a fool,

Is not so, Mr. Salt, in despite of his jaws.   ·

In the Heaven of letters he sings psalms to our sainted,

Gives pills in our critico-purgative school,

And is Master of Arts and a Doctor of Laws.

Salt. What 's his name?

        Anic. Sus Minervam.

                Salt. A great one.

                        Anic. A beater!

Sus. And pray what is yours?

        Salt. Mine is simple Saltpeter.

Sus. That 's *The cart draws the horse.*

As we say it in Latin,

Bovem' trahit currus: but ox falls less pat in.

Peter Salt, not Salt Peter, I take it of course.

Salt. No, it is as I tell you.

        Sus. Then *Salt,* I opine,

Was the name of your mother.

        Salt. No mother was mine.

Sus. Then your father's.

        Salt. I had none.

        Sus. A foundling, ha, ha!

A bastard?

        Salt. If 't please you.   Like others, I know not

The source of my being, though not blind to my true lot.

For aught that I know, I might claim for papa
That doughty Apostle whose thin blade 't is said
Circumcis'd Malchus' ear
Without shaving his head.

Sus. You mean your papa's oldtime foresire, 't is clear.
As his name too was Simon,
That 's a poor stock to climb on,
And, without amphibology,
Your Scripture chronology
Has been, Mr. Salt, much neglected, I fear.

Salt. Be that as it may,
This truly I say:
Like yourselves, I came into this world without will;
But, unlike yourselves, when I find I 've my fill,
I shall haste to go out of it, of my accord,
So soon as my governor whispers the word.

Sus. Who is your governor? 'T is not the Lord?
You don't look so pious.

                Anic. No, to judge by his eye,
One would think some one else had his Saltship for ward.

Sus. I like him for that; that fire would imply
He 's a deuse of a fellow.

                Salt. I am. Will you try?
I work on long credit; sometimes gratis, you 'll find.
Does it suit, who my governor is never mind.
You will both of you know him at no distant day.
He keeps long accounts, and, as you 've seen by the sample,
Has taught me to follow his princely example,
And be not exacting for present pay.

Sus. You 're a jewel of a man, Peter Salt or Salt Peter.
Let us strike up a bargain.
              Anic. My girls call me out.
I 'll be back to you soon. [*going.*
         Sus. [*aside.*] Salty dear, don't entreat her
To stay with us. Both will do better without.
                    [*Exit Anic.*
You must know —— Don't betray me !
           Salt. No, word of a devil !
Sus. What an oath ! What an odd fish you are !
                  You must know,
Our lady-friend's intellect 's under the level :
She is not an A.M., as I was long ago, —
(I 'm a Doctor of Laws too, my Quarterlies show.)
Therefore put off on *her* all your flatness and drivel,
If you have of those articles much to dispense.
Salt. Sus Minerv', LL.D., I would not be uncivil,
But, except when I practice a little deception,
They are products to which I can make no pretence.
Sus. They belong to the Dailies, I know, by prescription,
And to Minor-Note Fledgling by eminence.
Salt. There was some, it is true, in the piece I last sent you,
(I own it to show I would not circumvent you ;)
But in future I 'll give you misrepresentation,
 · Mock learning, bad syntax, and word-ostentation,
A truly illogical argumentation,
With a sparkle too of vituperation ;
And o'er all and through all, and 'mid scintillation,
Shall lie an amusing want of sense.

Sus. Dear Mr. Salt ! As from sympathy
　　You serv'd her for nothing, you will do this for me ?

Salt. I will do it, dear Doctor, because it will be
　　For my governor's delectation.

Sus. And for nothing?

　　　　　　　Salt. For nothing. But this is to say :
　　Better count the cost before we commence.
　　Though I charge not, the Devil may be to pay.

Sus. I am us'd to that in a general way :
　　So make haste, and damn the expense.

Salt. But in all that I promise you flourish already.
　　Mac'te virtu'te ; be bold and be steady.

Sus. Ha, ha, you have learning ! That is a new charm in you.
　　I will make you my partner !

　　　　　　　Salt. I should prove rather warm for you.
　　I use all the tongues of civilization
　　By an anti-apos'tolic inspiration, —
　　And certain more beside.
　　But let us return to my observation,
　　From which we are straying wide.
　　You have in yourself all you ask me to give;
　　But I 'll make you in letters the top of the nation,
　　And your name for ever to live.

Sus. How, how, how ?

Salt. Meet me about a half-hour from now.

Sus. Say where ! O where ?

Salt. In the Park, at the side on Slanghouse-Square.
　　I will introduce you to two friends there
　　Who will teach you to prick up your ears in the air.
　　　　Vol. ·IV.—19

Sus. I 'm the happiest dog beyond compare!

Salt. Hush! here comes the old sow.

    Be off now.

        Sus. Bow, wow!

> *Sus gets upon all fours,*
> *makes a demi-wheel on his hands, and Exit*
> *yelping delightedly.*

ACT THE THIRD [15]

SCENE. *The Park fronting Slanghouse-Square.*

Enter

ATTICUS, HEARTANDHEAD *and* GALANTUOM.

Gal. Here lies my street, at the right.   Let us stop.
Att. But not, for awhile yet, the question drop.
  Have you ever redd *Cato?*
                    Gal. To wonder and laugh.
More than half is mere prose.
                    Att. And the rest of it chaff.
There is nothing of nature in all, and the poet,
If conscious of passion, was unable to show it.
A schoolboy had written his love-scenes as well.
To affect to compare then *Virginia* with *Cato,*
Which has scarce one good part, save the passage on Plato,
To name Rowe and Young, and the public to tell
That our author was tutor'd in this or that school
Is to read without books.
                    Gal. Or to talk like a fool.
Why our tragedy-scribe, as the pert lady styles him
Who does up the Ethnos' old linen for new,
Has made his own school; though, while Round-Robins
  sell

And knaves that are Masters of Asses revile him,
He will have to wait long for a pupil or two.

Att. That is said very well.

In the teeth of the *prôneurs* of Swinburne and Ruskin,
He has dar'd to talk clearly, has taken from passion
Her stilts, and despite of prescription and fashion
Has refus'd to put monsters in sock or in buskin.
But not in his diction   ·
And sentiments merely
Makes he Nature his guide;
But in the connection
And sequence of incidents, where others clearly
Set nothing by space, be it little or wide,
And time with its intervals put quite aside.
And in costume not less,
In the manners and thought-modes which mark out each
    nation,
He has labor'd more faithfully such to express
Than any before him, without contestation,
Whate'er his success.
You, Galantuom, in your frank declaration,
Have sought to commend him as pure in his style.
I have honor'd him more.
He has swept clean the Stage which was filthy before,
And made men be merry without being vile.
Which is something still better, and I think more sublime,
Than his lifting his tones without word-ostentation
And compressing his Acts in the limits of time.

Heart. The *Round Robin* labor'd, knew not what to do.

Its conscience prick'd sore, but the author was new.
So it *damn'd with faint praise*, and, with impudent leer,
Affecting the gracious, *taught others to sneer*.

Gal. For the trait you mention,
That impudent air of condescension,
Which must have made our poet smile,
And reminded him of the plate where you see
Beside a mastiff a little cur sitting
On a footing of borrow'd equality,
With an air of consequence the while,
Which says as might words, if words were fitting,
"Don't mind that big fellow, but look at me.
I patronize him. To a certain degree
You may let him have your attention." ——

Heart. I remember the print; the inscription redd,
"Impudence and Dignity."
Had the artist the *Round Robin* in his head,
Feeling big, and trying to look full-bred,
With its little rump near *Calvary ?*

Gal. Well, so far as the trait you mention,
That funny assumption of condescension,
I am with you, but not in the good intention
You seem to assign that pretentious sheet.
Yet, in its preposterous conceit
It tells us serenely it holds him no poet!
Then quotes and misquotes, and, in order to show it,
Makes none of its righteous selections complete,
For fear that its readers should scent out the cheat!

Heart. You forget one act of liberal dealing.

It has honor'd the Devil, who is great in oration,
With a good long piece of declamation,
Which, it says, is the nearest to demonstration
The author makes of poetic feeling.

Gal. A piece of satirical reasoning ! blent
With the kind of brimstone sentiment
At vogue in the underground dominion !
In rhyme too !

      Att. No doubt with a double intent, –
The style of the drama to misrepresent,
And offend the public opinion.
Had he been a true critic, he would have known,
However lofty may be its tone,
Impassion'd, pathetic, pointed or strong,
To dialogue Nature has rarely lent
What is call'd poetical ornament.
The noblest masters of tragic song
Have shunn'd it as shuns our author, and he,
By this truth of art and consistency,
May reap honor late, but will keep it long.

Gal. So I said, when extolling, what fools decry'd,
Those two first comedies of his.
His adherence to nature will not be deny'd
By those who know what nature is.
But Heartandhead differs.

      Heart. Not I indeed ;
Those are main points in my critical creed.
But I think the Round Robin err'd not of will,
But spoke to the best of his knowledge and skill,

With the grandly unconscious droll conceit
In letters of all such empirics;
For we find him assign
The afflatus divine;
Which he could not feel breathe in a single line
Of our author's most polish'd drama,
Where think you? (it is to take by its bleat
A bob-tail sheep for a lama)
To — oh the amazement! and oh the fun!
To travesty-singing Conington,
Who makes the lord of hexameter verse
His stately and deep-mouth'd epic rehearse
In *Marmion's* four-foot lyrics.
This shows that, though better in sense and breeding
Than Flunky Weathercock's scribbling-man,
Robin knows not what poetry is, and the plan
With its incongruity exceeding
Was nothing strange to the purblind possessor
Of respect for an Oxford Latin-professor.

Gal. All which is true.
But, beginning to quote what well he knew
Was both lofty in tone and ornate too,
Why did he stop? Because intent
To keep from the light his false argument. [16]

Heart. Yet he gave, spread out to the public view,
A foremost passage.
   Gal. Ah! did he so?
Your own kind nature makes you slow
To detect, beside ignorance, malice.

Quem-Deus-vult-perdere reckon'd o'er
The fourteen true verses, then stupidly chose
To invite their contrast with Knowles's four
Of vulgar, half-rythmical, fustian prose ;
No doubt to our poet's amus'd delight,
For he took the pains both pieces to cite
In a note to his story of *Alice.* [17]

Heart. I fear you are right.

Att. Yet you, Heartandhead, in a just cause have done
More to baffle these fools than of us either one,
Although you have done it in vain.
Galantuom wrote honestly, therefore well,
But he did but his duty in his vocation.
And on me a like obligation fell
In a different situation.
I fulfill'd it too ; but in part with pain ;
As could not but be,
Since I hold the theme of *Calvary*
Too awful for human brain.
But you, Heartandhead, who had given up long
The critic's function wherein you were strong,
As declare both Poe and Irving,
Without hope of renown took up agen
Your kindly and truthful and graceful pen,
To write back these false or misguided men
To the path from which they were swerving.
But the *Nightly Pillar* was deaf as a post. —

Heart. Or something worse, for it kept me tost
On hopes and doubts, afraid to say nay,

Yet loath to assent, till, my patience lost,
And asham'd to be put off day by day,
I told him my mind, and in sheer disgust
Took the manuscript bugbear away.
It was worse however with Weathercock's olio;
For Flunky is master; the youth is not,
Who does small chars for the dames of Hotchpot
In the *Nightly Pillar's* folio.
Flunky stammer'd and shuffled, and talk'd of space;
Yet my piece was brief, but in eulogy,
Which did not with his views agree,
Although I gave him to understand
The poet had never seen my face.

Gal. I think it might have alter'd the case,
Had you gone with cash in hand.

Heart. Not with Flunky.

      Gal. I know not that: the men
Who daily damn souls, for simple gain,
By their lust-tales and calls to abortion,
Would scarce be affected by shame or with pain,
That a critical piece by a classical pen
Should pay in their sheets its proportion.

Att. Well? He stammer'd and shuffled — revolving, no doubt,
How, an old acquaintance, he might get out
Of the mesh of your application.
'T is the Weathercock's weakness, as is known,
To vibrate, by opposite winds when blown,
On his pivot of gyration.

Heart. And to turn over patiently stone after stone,
 19*

To explain his tergiversation.

Gal. Why true; but he 's quite outdone in that
By the greasy saint in the old white hat,
Who is like Val Jean in the *Misérables*, —
Who, liken'd to Christ in the strife for good,[18]
Yet tries more tricks to get out of the wood
Than any beast in Fontaine's *Fables*.

Att. Well, — he shuffled and stammer'd and talk'd of space ——

Heart. To consider how best he might with grace
Refuse.

   Gal. Which must have made you smile
For a half-breed of the mongrel journals,
Us'd to the haste,
The scissors and paste,
Of his piebald minute-liv'd diurnals,
To choke at an essay of yours.

      Heart. Meanwhile,
The poet got wind of my design,
Through a mutual friend, and thinking, 't may be,
Qui facit per alium facit per se,
Begg'd, that for his sake, as well as mine,
I would withdraw it definitively.

Gal. 'T was a false pride, I think.

      Att. No, he who wrought
Virginia, and thinks what his Ernestin taught,
Could do no less, it appears to me.

Heart. But is it not strange, this hostility
In the hounds of the Press?

      Gal. 'T is a personal quarrel.

Who wrote *Rubeta* and *Arthur Carryl*

Deserv'd no mercy, you must confess.

Head. Not had he libel'd by falsehood, as they.

Gal. " The greater the truth, the worse the libel."

To prove your foes false, yet in what you say

Be yourself the Bible,

Is to turn on their foulness the glare of day.

Att. But who of these asses first open'd the bray

Gal. The *Ethnos'* old lady, who spins a long yarn.

Then the Master of Asses himself, who, they say,

Buys all her old fodder to store in his barn.

The result is so like, not alone in the strain

Of shameless untruth, but assumption vain,

They have had the same devil at work, 't is plain,

Whoever may be to pay.

Heart. Let us go to the *Ethnos* and find how it is.

Att. I 'm not known ——

      Heart. But I am to the petticoat quiz.

'T is worth the essay.

Come, Gal'ant.

      Gal. Not now. As I told you, yon street,

Where the *Civis* is, calls me away.

But, in less than an hour, I will both of you meet

At Anicula's.

      Heart. Well then.

        Gal. Good day.

ACT THE FOURTH

SCENE. *As in Act III.*

SUS. SALTPETER. BRIMSTONE. CHARCOAL.

Salt. These are my friends. Let me make you known.
Gentlemen, this is the great A.M. ——
Sus. And LL.D.
   Salt. And LL.D.,
Who by natural right of his double degree,
And that alone ——
Sus. No, my Quarterly.
Salt. And his quarterly sheet of motley knowledge,
 To learning and letters makes more pretence
 With an infinitesimal dose of sense,
 Than was ever yet made, or will be hence,
 Out of a Freshman's class at college.
 Doctor Sus Minervam.
     Sus. Gentlemen both,
I am not at all proud, being us'd to praise, —
So am happy to make your acquaintance. Though loath,
Permit me first a question to raise.
What are your names? Mr. Salt forgot,
Too full of me, and my titles God wot,
To name the characters in his plot.

Salt. This gentleman then, with the fiery nose,
 Is Mr. Brimstone, dull quiet stuff,
 If he only would keep cool enough;
 But he is very apt to get blue.
 The other in the iron-gray clothes,
 And with so swart a hue,
 Is a light and spongy fellow, like you,
 Yet with a fibre you can't see through,
 Though neither solid nor tough.
 His name is Charcoal.
    Sus. And yours Saltpeter!
 With such a three,
 It appears to me,
 Unless you 're a most outrageous cheàter,
 It hardly is safe to keep company.
Salt. That might be in another place.
 But here, unless you carry fire,
 You 're as safe as you would be in the mire
 Of your own journal's dirtiest place.
Sus. That is safe enough; for I scarcely can keep,
 When I bogtrot there, my brains from sleep,
 And I get stuck fast, with big words and grammar,
 As often as waddling Anicula (d — n her!)
Salt. And now to business. But first, a word.
 Have you faith, Dr. Sus,
 That the spirit-world ever comes to us, —
 I mean to the men of this earth, — as averr'd?
Sus. By whom?
    Salt. By hysterical girls who are able

To talk with ghosts through the planks of a table
And see through the mop of their chignons.

           Sus. Absurd !

Salt. You don't believe then ?

        Sus. A question for me !
You forget I am a double L. D.
I believe, Mr. Salt, in all that I see.
All the rest,
That will not admit of this ocular test,
Mental or real, is — fiddlededee.

Salt. Some years now gone,
    Your great fool of a credulous town
    Got raving Irish-mad with joy,
    Because John Bull with your townsman's aid,
    For his people's sake and not your own,
    Beneath the ocean a means had laid
    To make by a flash his two shores as one
    And some day work to your annoy.
    Do you doubt the flash ? Well, you see it not.

Sus. But I know its result.

        Salt. And as much might be said
Of the visit of ghosts to this spot.
But my friends will do more.
You shall not only hear as the media do
The ghosts of the dead, but shall see them too,
As Saul did priest Samuel's of yore.

Sus. Do you deal with the Devil ?

        Salt. No; don't you see
How vers'd I am in Scripture lore ?

It is the Devil who deals with me.

Sus. Don't take me for one you can play your tricks on,
    Like Ferdinand Mendez Pinto Dixon,
    Who found the female American nation,
    On a single married *lady's* confession,
    Committing puerperal repression [19]
    By philosophical calculation,
    And because his apples were munch'd by one,
    Who found them more succulent than her own,
    Wish'd, for them all, that he might imbue 'em
    With the moral meaning of *meum* and *tuum*.

Salt. I see you can tell the truth sometimes.

Sus. When it does n't jar with my vocation,
    And thereby diminish the dollars and dimes,
    But what is that to our present relation?
    You would have me believe I can see without eyes.

Salt. Let not that surprise.
    How do you know that you see at all?
    How many are with me here?
                   Sus. Why, two.

No, Mr. Brim has slipp'd from view.

Brim. Bah! I am here all the while, nor so small
    But that you might see, if you really saw.

Sus. Then you stepp'd behind your fellow.
                      Brim. Nor that
    Not the toe of my boots nor the crown of my hat,
    The hairs on my chin, nor the tips of my paw.

Sus. Then you are the Devil.
                  Brim. I never bore

My swallow-tail'd pennant yet so high
As the great three-decker who was of yore
The Lord High Admiral of the sky.
I may be though a devil for aught you know.
But that is nothing to you, I trow,
So that we pay the debt we owe
And make you see what you doubted before.

Sus. And keep your promise?

            Salt. What else? Your head
Shall be a more than nine days' wonder,
And men who pay no regard to thunder
Shall do it reverence instead.

Sus. Before I die?

        Salt. And after too.
No man, as I said,
Nor of the living nor of the dead,
Shall prick up his ears as high as you.

Sus. But say, Mr. Salt, when shall this be?
Say where? O where? that I shall see
That new-fangled tail to my double degree ·
Which shall lift me up ——

          Salt. Asinauricularly ——

Sus. With my ears prick'd up
Like a terrier-pup ——

Salt. But longer ——

       Sus. In perpetuity.

Salt. Ay, when the Griswolds and Duyckincks are rotten,
And all you have squirted yourself is forgotten,
Save one divine article

Of which not a particle
Shall be lost to the last of the Yankees begotten,[20]
Your name and your ears
Shall escape the old shears
Which, with rhymsters, is set to the thread of man's years,
And your skull shall as now be begetter of jeers
When its insides are out like a herring's that 's shotten.

Sus. O delight! O the joy! O dearest of dears,
    O Salty, say when is this prospect to be?

Salt. When it suits you to talk less and trot after me.

Sus. And where? Say where!

Salt. On the other side of Slanghouse-Square;
    Where Anicula's lasses
    Soft-soap the asses,
    And do for the masses
    Other journalistic drudgery.

Sus. But we shall be seen.

Salt. What matters? She was our go-between.
    Would you have your glory unnoted, unknown?

Sus. Set on!
    With all your combustible matter in one.
    Though all three were ramm'd,
    Brimstone, Saltpeter and Charcoal, together—
    It don't suit the jaws
    Of a Doctor of Laws
    To swear — but I 'm d—d
    If I 'd mind your blow-up more than that of a feather.
    Set on! set on!
    With you, gunpowder three,

Or with you alone,
Mr. Salt, I 'll see,
This night, this fun.
Be it ghost or devil,
Or both or one,
To-night I 'll revel
In the feast of my fame,
Or may my short name
Still shorter be
Of its single A.M. and its double L.D.,
On the front backside of my Quarterly.
Charge, Brimstone, *charge! on*, Charcoal, *on*
To the Devil, or victory !

Kicks over an astonished bootblack,
and Exit in a fit of enthusiasm,
followed by the three with various gestures of
admiration.

ACT THE FIFTH

SCENE. *Anicula's Sanctum, as in Act II.*

SALTPETER. CHARCOAL. BRIMSTONE.

Brim. What keeps the fool ?
     Salt. Our LL.D. ?
Brim. The Lord of the *Ethnical Quarterly.*
Salt. In his haste to reach the rendezvous,
 The goose fell foul of an apple-wench,
 Upset her pippins, herself and bench,
 And got for himself in the kennel a drench
 Of the savory stew
 The Hotchpotian Irish corporation
 Keep mix'd for the people's delectation,
 But which to the nostrils of me and you,
 Who are us'd to the ashes and sulphurous smell
 That thicken the air round the craters of Hell
 Where the fires burn blue,
 Is a damnable abomination.
 So, holding my nose, I left him there,
 Lock'd in the claws of the dirt-mobled fair,
 Both kicking and swearing,
 And each other's clothes tearing,
 Two human beasts in a worse than beast's lair.

Brim. I suppose we shall have to await his cleaning ?

Salt. By Lucifer! yes, he will need repair
    After his pomologic careening.
    He is well pay'd already with kitchen-pitch,
    Both body and breech,
    And will get of calking more than he lists
    From the iron fingers and mallet fists
    Of the shipwright he dubb'd an Hibernian bitch.

Brim. When he rights on his keel and floats in here,
    We will rig him with standing and running gear
    In such a wise ——

Char. His bowsprit at least,
    With its figurehead beast ——

Brim. As will make old seamen blast their eyes.

Salt. We shall give him his desert, in sooth.
    And here a contradiction lies :
    We have punish'd the bard for telling truth,
    The true in art, and in morals true,
    And now we shall make the critic rue
    His false instruction and peddling lies.

Brim. But lo, where he comes !

Enter Sus.

       Salt. What has kept you so long?

Sus. The hussy was strong.
    Before I cut loose
    From her kedge in the gutter
    The bloody Philistin,

With her great raw-meat fist in

My joles, while I utter,

In distraction, a volley of tragic abuse, —

And that not in Latin,

Though the slang came quite pat in,

From my quarterly use, —

The uncircumcis'd jade ——

Salt. Uncircumcis'd?

               Sus. Ay. Don't balk my narration.

— Demands to be paid —

Judge my rage, consternation!

For her codlings that swim — not in buttery juice.

Was *I* not too coddled? and in the same stuff?

'T was a shame! 't was a fraud! But afraid of the trollop,

Who continu'd to wollop

About me and made the mob jolly enough,

I agreed, when half-deafen'd, and after ado,

To take for five nickels the nastiest two,

Then *skedaddled*, [21] got wash'd, and came limping to you.

Salt. 'T was a Red-sea escape. You 're a Sampson, 't is plain.

Brim. With an ass's jawbone.

             Sus. Do not talk in that strain:

I 've no wish to be vain:

One Philistine like her, though, might count for a twain.

But you, Mr. Salt, are a nice friend in need!

Salt. Why, what could I do?

There were just of you two.

I thought you well pitted;

And as you were fitted —

Sus. You left me to bleed!

Humph! Let us proceed.

Salt. We are ready. Behold!   .

The blinds are down-roll'd.

Sus. And the candle burns blue.

The devil!

   Salt. Not yet.

He 'll not tread the scene till you get in his debt,

Though the flame has his hue.

Sus. Do turn on the gas, Mr. Salty, please do.

Salt. Doctor dear, do not fret.

When our drama is through,

And your glory completed, then light up the jet.

In this dimness the ghosts will come better in view.

Sus. Ghosts! Oh, dear me! where 's Anicula then?

Brim. She has crawl'd back into her inner den

To get her girls prudently out of the way.

The dame fain would stay,

Being jealous, and anxious to share in your glory,

And go down like you with great ears in men's story;

But we knew your ambition, and taught her she bare

Length enough in her own without clipping your pair.

But she soon will be back, I will venture to say,

From her eagerness in the affair.

Sus. Out on the jade! Such conduct sickens,

As much as the money-greed of Dickens

Who having, after his cockney mood,

Abus'd us by all the lies he could,

Is coming here for our Yankee pelf.

To make a greater ass of himself,
While we, like spaniels well broke-in,
Forget his thumps and vulgar curses,
And opening, like our hearts, our purses,
Beg him to help himself to our tin,
Then turn up our rumps
ˑFor more of his thumps,
And lick his toes till the kicks begin.

Salt. Eh, *Legum Doctor !* say you so ?
That is truth again.   Why, you advance !
He has not engag'd you, I see, to enhance
His low grimaces ?

       Sus. Who, Dickens ?   No.
The daily press are made fat instead,
As they always are when such feasts are spread.
We of the quarterlies sit too far
From the end of the board where the Flunkies are,
To come in for a share of the broken bread.
But let us begin.

Salt. Ere the dame comes in ?
With all my heart.

Brimstone *disappears, and arises an Apparition.*

What see you there?
Sus. With the large sad eyes and the youthful hair ?
His cheeks are pale and gaunt.   But what
Means here and there that discolor'd spot?
Salt. 'T is the livid mark of the poison he took ;

    The sole post-obit in his look.

Sus. O, I understand; and I know him wholly.

    No wonder he looks so rantipolly.

    'T is the ghost, by Jove, of Thomas Rowley!

Salt. But hist, till he speaks. If he leave in disdain,

    My friends may not waken him up again.

Appar. Great Master of Asses and LL.D.,

    What had I done that you libel'd me?

Sus. 'T is Brimstone's voice. But the ghost is well-bred.

    I see they have manners among the dead.

    Libel'd! I wrote in a laud-sounding strain.

    There is no "Shakspearian scholar" more hot

    In the love of his idol's most whimsical blunder,

    Or who takes his worst gong-beat for genuine thunder,

    Than I when resounding your praises, God wot.

Appar. 'T is of that I complain.

    Gapes there ever a fool

    Who is fresh from the rhetoric benches at school,

    But knows what sort of stuff you quote, —

    Although it was not all stuff I wrote?

    Is that the drama? And such its style?

    You have taught your readers to stare, or smile.

    That is not nature as now I know it,

    And praising my verses you damn'd the poet.

        Ghost vanishes, and reappears BRIMSTONE.

Sus. You are here again! Do you juggle so?

Brim. I but saw him down; which was right you know,

Since I tickled him up from his snooze below.

Sus. Oh ho!

Salt. Close up, old pup;

Another poet is sailing up.

Exit CHARCOAL, *and Apparition rises.*

Sus. His brick-red curls are sprinkled with snow.

His light eyes beam

With self-conceit, and a pleasant gleam

That is not the flash of the tragic storm.

And yet I would swear that lofty form,

With its lively face and expanded brow,

Is one I know, or ought to know.

Appar. Me, thou impertinent! know me, thou!

Thou mayst have sense in thy degree ——

Sus. In my double degree.

       Appar. Peace, vain fool!

Who thought of thy honors from college or school?

Despite thy A.M. ——

       Sus. And my double L. D.

Appar. Thou mayst have line enough to gage

The shoal still pool, where no tempests rage,

Of *the Spanish Student,* or measure *Queechy,*

Not the depths of *Filippo* or *Polini'ce.*

Sus. That terrible voice is Charcoal's own,

Though ten times louder, and haughty in tone.

I know him now, with his scalp so hairy

And whiskerless jaws. It is Count Alfieri.

VOL. IV.—20

Appar. *Count* unto thee, whose envious hate
    Reproach'd me with pride in that titled lot
    Which by right of birth so natural sate
    On my father's name that I felt it not;
    But to the world my works still bore
    Victor Alfieri, and nothing more:
    A pride by you not understood,
    Who have stuck the letters of both your degrees,
    Cheap and unearn'd although they were ——

Sus. To that I demur;
    I paid for them twenty ——

                    Appar. Silence, cur! ——
    Have thrust each cheap, unearn'd degree,
    That men your sole claims to knowledge might see,
    On every side, wherever you could ——

Sus. No, Signor Contè, if you please,
    On the bare backside of my Quarterly,
    And with some of the Press, in notice or puff,
    Whom I patronize for a *quantum suff.*
    We do all things here for cash you know, —
    Though you go on tick, I suppose, below.

Appar. Silence, once more! —— That thou hast try'd,
    Thou to whom honor nor truth is known,
    To asperse my fame, who liv'd and dy'd
    Slave unto Truth, and Truth alone,
    This I forgive, though thou shalt atone
    To that public judgment thou hast defy'd.

Sus. Have mercy, good ghost, nor deprive me of bread:
    In my next I will take back all I have said, —

On the word of a critic, and as sure as you 're dead!

Appar. Hound! dar'st thou deem I am like thy tribe,

To cant or recant as men pay or bribe?

Thy aspersions are praise, and another pen

Shall make of them mirth for the gizzards of men.

But what I can neither forgive nor forget,

Until in the regions above I am set

Where men o'er their wrongs are not suffer'd to fret —

Sus. And no Minor critics condemn in a pet.

Appar. A pest on thy pestilent tongue! — What is worse,

I say, than thy praise, thou hast made me rehearse

As I never yet spoke, nor in prose nor in verse.

Unasham'd thou hast ventur'd to strip off the buskin

From the feet of my toga'd and chlamydate Tuscan,

And clap on the socks of thy English instead,

Slipshod, and soft as the pap of thy head.

Better in tinsel, cross-garter'd, to tread

With the stage-strut of Emerson, Carlyle and Ruskin.

Sus. *Peccavi! sed non mea culpa;* not mine

The soft worsted; I bought it at sixpence a line.

The all that I did was to lend it some picking:

I adopted the cub; but I gave him a licking.

Appar. Didst thou so? Now I 'm minded to give thee a kicking.

But the weakness or want of the flesh has come o'er me,

And Brimstone and Charcoal must do the job for me.

Apparition vanishes, and reappears CHARCOAL.

Sus. He has *vamos'd the ranch.*[22] And there 's Charcoal again!

This is all hocuspocus, or masking; that's plain.

Char. Not a whit. Do you think a sixfooter like him

Could step from his niche in the Shades, nor be miss'd?

Sus. Why, the chance were but slim.

Char. — So I took up his place in Probational Hell,

And escap'd all detection by means of its mist.

As for masking, how could a paste-board imitation

Be proof to the lens of your us'd penetration?

Sus. Very right, Mr. Coal. Vain to hope it. As well

Look for judgment in Greeley, or truth in the *Nation,*

Bid Raymond stand still for a minute, or Sedley

Tell more than he hides in his fortnightly medley.

Salt. What are those? Of the four, are unknown to me three.

Sus. One a coverless journal; the others are asses,

That mix, though unlike, as do milk and molasses,

And wake pity and mirth when they bray to the masses,

Like the *Ethnos* or me.

Salt. My friends now, great Doctor, have shown you their

power:

I have kept half my word; you know how ghosts look.

Will it do? Shall they summon up more? But the hour

Is late, and the dame will be leaving her nook.

Sus. No, give me the rest of your promise; I long

To wear my grand ears and be famous in song.

Salt. It is well: but not yet. You have shown yourself brave.

You are leag'd hand and glove with the servants of

Hell —

Sus. Not with you? [*in alarm.*

       Salt. Never mind. — And chop logic as well

With the pupæ whose sordid cocoon is the grave.

By these two acts alone,

Already you wear them.

But forever to bear them

And by them be known,

You must prove by your gifts they are truly your own.

Sus. By my gifts? How you prate! Am I not LL.D.,

And was A.M. before?

Then give them to me.

By the Powers ye adore,

By the shame I defy

Were it doubled twice o'er,

O Saltpeter, I cry,

Let me feel, ere I die,

`My long ears stand up somewhat nearer the sky!

Salt. Can you go through the proofs that shall make these gifts

known?

Sus. Through them all! Only try.

Salt. O hero!

  Sus. Be quick!

    Salt. On thy four paws go down.

And give him the halter. What! up? So soon scar'd?

Sus. I would hang for the ears; but my neck must be spar'd.

Neck or nothing.

    Salt. With us, it is nothing indeed.

To know you have patience, can keep your own way

Spite of coaxing or curses —

Save when flatter'd your greed

Is by dreams of full purses —

Nor, shamefac'd, will heed
The worst men may say,
This is all that we need.

Sus. That exception observ'd, which is wise nowadays
When a patron is valu'd for what he disburses,
The rest is as light as to spawn tadpole verses
Such as *Round-Robins* praise,
While Fledgling, who knows not which most to admire,
A jewsharp, or bagpipe, or Æolus' lyre,
But dotes on Walt Whitman's batrachian fire,[23]
Shall, in love with their long tails, the porwiggles feed
As full-breech'd green frogs of the Horse-fountain breed.

Salt. What! what! truth again? If you sing in this strain,
Your ears will be stretch'd to the ass point in vain.

Sus. Never fear: I but stumble thus trotting alone,
Or with friends; in my journal I rein-in my roan,
And decide by my belly and not by my brains.

Salt. True metal! But quick; on your quarters once more.
How the halter becomes him! Now clap on the pack.
While Charcoal sits woman-wise perch'd on his back,
You, Brim, jerk his tail, while I drag him before.

Sus. But don't jerk so hard, or my tail will be torn.
'T is my best workday-coat and is only half-worn.
And don't kick so much. Ow! ow!

                                     Salt. If you cry,
You 'll have more than the dame bouncing in to know why.

Sus. O my! O my!
O my seat of honor!
Pray, don't spank so hard! The dame — curse upon her!

Let me up! let me up! The dame — d—n the wench!

She sha' n't see me stretch'd like a washermaid's bench.

Salt. Do you pull up so soon?

> *Sus.* Up?   'T is you beat me down.

My rump 's not an ass's, whatever my crown.

Salt. But the ears?

> *Sus.* Let them go.   Ow! I 'm beat black and blue.

I can't carry Charcoal and bear your kicks too.

Salt. Let him rise.   It will do.

Sus. Do? my back 's almost broken.

Salt. You have prov'd it of steel.

And this is the token:

You have kept your own way

Like a genuine ass, — though with rather more bray.

Sus. But, for all that, I feel.

Now give me the ears.

> *Salt.* Not as yet.   You have shown,

It is true, soul and carcass, an ass's backbone.

You must now make it known

You can swing to the popular breath of the nation,

And to private dictation —

Sus. For a gratification —

Salt. To and fro with a prompt oscillation,

Or round with a gallowsbird's circumgyration,

Whatever the compass-point whence it is blown.

Sus. Pshaw! I do that with ease! Not Weathercock Flunky,

Though daily, more duly, nor his Topical monkey.

Salt. Let us see! Hang him up by his weasand.

> *Sus.* [*in alarm.*] What 's that!

I will not box the compass — save on paper, — that's flat!

Salt. But you must, or no ears. Fix the hook. Trice him up.
By the coat-collar only, you ninny.

      Sus. You 'll tear it.

Salt. But the glory, the ears!   Will you lose them, to spare it?

Sus. O me! I shall dangle just like a blind pup.

Salt. Or a sheep in the shambles.

      Sus. But whence come these things:
The hoop, and the ring in the ceiling, and block,
With the rope that thence swings?

Salt. They are brought by the phantoms on tables that knock.

Sus. Pheew!

      Salt. What, doubting? 'T is harder to hurl fiddles
round
On the sconces of gazers and make guitars sound
By invisible thumbs, as your Davenports do.

Sus. That is true.

Salt. As the ghosts of the verse-men we summon'd to view.
There.   Up with him! oo!

Sus. Oh, oh! let me down!   Let me down, or I 'll cry!
My brains are aswound.
My heels kiss the ceiling
And my skull treads the ground.
I don't know which is which while my brainpan keeps
reeling
And my navel goes round.

      They unhook him.

Salt. So.   You have learn'd vacillation.

Sus. I knew it of yore,

While you slabber'd your mother, or even I trow
Were coil'd up a *fœtus in utero*,
To your daddy's delectation.

Salt. You practic'd then shifting, some ages or more
Ere the Spirit that brooding sat over the deep
Put the breathing red clay in his consciousless sleep,
To produce an equivocal first generation.

Sus. Oh horror! I 'm hous'd with the Father of Sin,
Or one of his kin.

Salt. With neither. But what if you were, so you win?
Set your heart on the ears,
And your feet on these fears;
Your fame shall grow younger while olden the years.

Sus. Enough. Shall I more? Through the Devil and Hell
I would stride to my glory. Push onward.

       Salt. 'T is well.

You must next learn false candor.

      Sus. I avow that in that

Round Robin 's my master.

     Salt. He needs not to be.

You have only to hide what is lofty as he,
And vaunt to the skies the ignoble or flat.

Sus. I do! I do!
Witness your ghosts if I do not speak true.

Salt. But to make that appear,
You must perch on your head with your claws in the air.

Sus. O spare! O spare!
Set me down, set me down!
All the blood leaves my seat to descend to my crown.
 20*

Set me down, or I 'm dead:

My brain is afire, my eyes flame; I 'm sped!

O my soul!

Salt. [*righting him.*   ✱

You are all over red.

'T is the dawn of your triumph.

Sus. No, the set of my pole.

I hope this is all.

   Salt. Not enough for your fame.

The next thing to learn is the goodbye to shame.

Sus. I have bid it already. Attest that, my Quarterly.

Not inside alone, but without, as you ought to see,

It is printed in full.

   Salt. Where your name is. We know it.

But off with your breeches, and caper to show it.

Sus. There.

Brim, let them down tenderly, else they will tear.

Ye gods, I am bare!

Salt. Let us chant.

   Sus. Well, begin.

Salt. Now, Doctor, keep time.

   Sus. And, in time, if the air

Suit my taste, I 'll chime in.

  Salt. *In puris naturalibus,*

   The Doctor's dainty legs discuss

   The lines of beauty, capering thus,

   As if he 'd pass'd at Willis'.[21]

Sus. The air however 's rather cool.
　　I think you make me play the fool,
　　Too plump for nature's dancingschool,
　　With short *tendo Achillis.*

Brim. Give him a kick, to spin him round;
Char. Another, for the pair that 's found
　　Of cushions waiting their rebound.
Salt. But spring a little higher.

Sus. I would the world could see my shame,
　　Who caper thus for future fame —
Salt. As David, when he 'd won the game
　　Of Jack-stones with Goliah.

Sus. Yet stop! though dancing does agree
　　With naked tibial dignity,
　　It hardly suits my Quarterly,
　　Although it saves my breeches.

　　Besides, my breath is growing short.
Salt. And, Doctor, you have made good sport,
　　A Sampson in Philistine court,
　　As *Judges* XV. teaches.

Sus. How well you know the sacred text!
Salt. It is my forte ; and Henry Beecher
　　Himself might be perhaps perplex'd,

Although a most accomplish'd preacher,
To follow where my memory reaches,
And think perhaps that Satan preaches.

Sus. He often does, rude laics say.

I have known myself a broker pray,
And cheat his client the same day
And bring him to the verge of starving,
Say grace to his thanksgiving-dinner,
(His creditor had none, mean sinner!)
Then smile, as doubtless should the winner,
The while a sumptuous sirloin carving.
But have I done ?

    Salt. We pause, you see.

Char. First, accept these two love spanks,
Given, if with emotion rough,
One on each cheek, yet tenderly.

Sus. One for both were caress enough.

Yet for the gift I render thanks.

Char. And ought, for your hide is beastly tough.

Sus. 'T is sitting so long at my task ev'ry quarter.

'T would harden the beef of an alderman's daughter.

Char. Or of Brimstone. or me.

Sus. I have danc'd and sung, and I feel ecstatic
From fundament to Mansard attic.
I would there were no more to do,
Than shake a leg with Salt and you.
But help me now my drawers indue :
Their want gives over much to view,
And makes me seem erratic.

I only wish the dullard crew,
Who make pretensions to review
The poets they can scarcely read,
Would dance like me in cuerpo once
'T would fire the liver of each dunce,
And, acting on his brain-pulp, serve
To make him guess at tragic verve.
Please hold my drawers awhile, while now
I wipe the dewdrops from my brow
Of wholesome perspiration.
I do not like to swear, yet vow,
With shirt and jacket on and coat,
Cravatted too, but *sans culotte*,
I 'm like the bird that talks by rote
Bi-monthly in *the Nation*.
Come, give the calicos.

     Salt. Not yet.

As 't is convenient, let us set
His titles on his naked parts,
Laws' Doctor and great man of Arts.

Sus. M. stands for Master, not Man, Mister.

Char. So brand it *Artium Magister.*

Bring the iron that sears.

Sus. No, no! by my tears!
Make me not a freemason — at least not for life!
If the brand should be seen! —— Have regard for my
  wife.

Salt. He has suffer'd enough,
  And has prov'd the right stuff.

Let us give him the ears.

Sus. O joy!

　　　Salt. Hold your tongue: it is greatly too long.

Sus. And a long tongue licks up vexation.

　　You forget my degrees and might have spar'd me the wrong

　　Of that vocative mortification.

Salt. Well, hush then, great Doctor, and listen the song, —

　　While you, Brimstone and Charcoal,

　　Stop with spittle each earhole,

　　And rub up, nor mind the pain ——

Sus. Yes, yes; for mine the pain.

Salt. — The rims, till they shine again, —

　　The song of our Incantation.

　　But first, though you have prov'd a wonder

　　In bestial worth, and may defy

　　Compare, yet this is to supply:

　　You must tread conscience wholly under,

　　Boldly dash and never blunder,

　　Ere your ears will reach the sky.

Sus. Then crown the work, nor more deny

　　My honors; nought is to be fear'd;

　　My conscience is already Sear'd.

　　Save Deadhead sole and Flunky's Fledgling,

　　I know not any moral ridgling

　　Can sense and decency defy,

　　Suppress the truth, or boldly lie,

　　With such indifference as I.

Salt. Well then, attend; and while Coaly and Brim

　　Bespittle your holes and chafe each ear-rim,

Make no outcry.

By the spirits in darkness dwelling,
Styebak'd, half-naked, and wholly obscene;
By the thick oils from underground welling,
Making naptha and kerosene; —

Sus. What a queer charm!
Salt. If you 'd not come to harm,
You will take good care not to cross my spelling.

By the sheet-lightning, that dazzles, not kills,
Image of force that is only in seeming;
By the miasms from stagnant pools steaming,
Filling men's vitals with fever and chills;

By the town-council in mud that reposes,
Shellfish that neither are oyster nor clam,
By their vile gutters that reck not of roses,
Making the taxpayers frown, spit and damn;

Sus. And press hard their noses.
Salt. Will you hold?
Sus. Having roll'd
But just now in that clover,
1 have study'd its botany over and over,
And thought I might add, as a note, 'T is no sham.
But be quick; for my auricles are glowing;

And my digits can't find out at all that they. 're growing.
Salt. Patience and list.   When the charm is all sung.
　　Your ears will have almost the stretch of your tongue.

　　　　By all that is vile, or in nothingness ending,
　　　　Borrow'd and full of pretension vain,
　　　　Come with your tails up, straight, corkscrew'd, and
　　　　　　bending,
　　　　Creatures that symbol his heart and his brain:

　　　　Monkey and magotpie, paddock and frog,
　　　　And spitting she-kitten and snarling cur-dog,
　　　　Reremouse, and nyctalopic owl,
　　　　Crocodile grim, and hyena fowl, —
　　　　His arts' eido'la and types of his mind,
　　　　Surround him, caress him; he is of your kind.

Sus. O me! O me!   I wish I was blind.
　　The owl 's on my head.
　　And the monkey —— You imp, take your paws off!
　　　Let go;
　　Or you 'll strangle me.   Oh!
　　And that beast from the Nile,
　　With his amplify'd smile,
　　His yard-long mouth — scissors and chopper and file,
　　Keep him back, or I 'm dead.
Salt. O fi! O fi!
　　A Doctor, and cry?

These spirits, though evil,
Will give health to your navel,
Not make you to die.
They will teach you to mimic, — to prate without mean-
 ing, —
To stare without seeing, — to puff without pride, —
To feign frozen chastity,
While in hot nastity
Seeking by harsh words lust-itching to hide, —
To growl o'er the stript bones you're savagely cleaning, —
To tear from their graves and disfigure the dead, —
To be daz'd with the twilight,
Half mouse and half sparrow,
And dash, like an arrow
Misshot, through a skylight, —
To croak with facility
The tuneless un-sense of a sapless anility, —
And give you ability
By a shrewd crocodility
To make shoddy seem broadcloth in all you have said.
In fine, they will stuff, with goëtic agility,
Your brainpot with feathers and your heart's pipes with
 lead.

Sus. The dear ugly creatures! Each fright is a fairy.
I feel my ears prick, my os frontis grows hairy.
O Stoney, O dear Coal,
Spit your best at each ear-hole,
Nor of friction be chary.
O feathers and lead !

Ah feathers and lead !

You were wrong, noble Salty, in what you last said :

My head 't is grows heavy, my heart that is airy.

O, O !

I wish I could show

My crown to all Hotchpot at once.   Let me go.

But the phantoms are leaving.   Goodbye, my dear
creatures.

The valves of my heart shall shut-in your sweet features ;

Especially yours, armor'd Earl of the Nile,

With your skillet-handle tail and your waffle-iron smile.

Adieu ! adieu ! —

Now, my rubbers, to you,

Whose hands have the magic of Moses,

I turn and demand,

Is there aught in this land

Can compare with my metamorpho'sis ?

Char. It is all very well ; a good head of its kind.

Sus. Good ?   'T is complete in each elegant feature,

And fits me like a second nature.

Char. And there is the very fault I find :

'T is too natural far.

It makes you appear,

Jaws, forepiece and ear,

Without counting the hair,

Like the ass that you are.

Sus. Say, donkey : it fits not my bifold degree

To be nam'd, though mark'd, asinauricularly.

But seem I the same ?

And if I be known by that recogniz'd name,
Which is Fledgling's and Deadhead's
And some other leadheads',
I who have run the whole college curriculum,
Why what upon earth shall cognominate me?
Char. *Asinor'um Magis'ter, Lectōrum' Deridic'ulum.*
Sus. Why, that is my A.M. and double L. D.!
But here is Anicula. Now we shall see.

Enter ANICULA.

Anic. Eh! Bottom the weaver!
Now, would I were Titania for thy sake.
I 'd "kiss thy fair large ears, my gentle joy."
Sus. Dost think I 'd hug a doxy of your make?
I would as soon buss Fledgling, or a boy.
But oh thou deceiver! [*gaily to Salt.*
If one may believe her,
Who 's as false as *the Nation,*
She at least, 't would appear,
Is fully aware
Of my beautiful transfiguration.
For this I adore thee,
And could kneel down before thee,
And aye ready to serve am.
Anic. Sure, 't is old Sus Minervam!
That fools-voice reveal'd him,
As the dim light conceal'd him.
Pray, let me explore thee.

Why, you 're perfect, I vow.
Feels it good?

        Sus. Bless the maker,
'T is my soul's simulachre:
I never had justice till now.

Anic. Mr. Salt, give me one. —
But your candle burns dim.

Salt. Ancient dame, you need none. —
Light the gas, Mr. Brim.

Sus. He does 't with his fingers! Is the devil in him?

Salt. No, on my veracity,
'T is his Brimstone capacity.
He has the felicity
To use electricity
Like matches, for fun.

Anic. But again for the ass-head. Why don't I need one?

Salt. It would make you less trim.
And, as simple Anicula,
In your function particular
You give quite as droll delectation,
By your senile garrulity
And anile credulity ——

Sus. As if you were chief of *the Nation.*
But here come two witlings, to heighten my joy, —
Though one is a monkey;
Polyphemus's boy
And the turnspit of Flunky.
I 'll play mum and enjoy their surprise.

Enter DEADHEAD *and* FLEDGLING.

Dead. Old lady, your humble contumble.   My eyes !
  What a mask !
        Fledg. And what size !
  I will make on 't a note for my *Topics.*
  We don't breed such at home.
  Whence can the beast come ?
Dead. From Aspis, I think, in the Tropics.
  Anic', you she-monkey,
  Get on the old donkey.
Sus. No you don't.
        Fledg. Eh ! 't is Sus.
  Who gave him those ears ?
Anic. Mr. Salt, it appears ;
  Or, it may be, the Devil.
Fledg. Fi, old woman, be civil.
  Give them, wise man, to us.
Sus. Be off, and don't trouble him.
  They are mine, and mine only.
Salt. Fear not, I can't double them ;
  Though, your asshead's not lonely.
Fledg. Can we make no conditions ?   I feel we shall die,
  If outdone by the Doctor, Mort-Caput and I.
Anic. What stuff !   Don't I stand in my petticoat by ?
Sus. Well protested, old dame of the *Ethnos ;* but higher
  Than greatness soars envy, as smoke above fire.
Salt. Notwithstanding, these witlings shall have their desire.
Fledg. How ?

Dead. Say how !

Salt. By leaving your birth-marks to stand just as now ;
    Only making each feature
    Better photograph nature,
    As with the great Doctor, on jaw, nose and brow.

Dead. Begin then, begin.

Fledg. But is it not sin ?

Dead. Out, sanctity ! Is n't there money to win ?
    Push on, jolly proctor,
    Make us grin like the Doctor,
    We 'll line you with greenbacks or plate you with tin.

Salt. Attend then.

        Sus. *Fave' te.*

           Fledg. That means, Stop your din.

Salt. Not from the spirit-world need we to summon
    Biped or quadruped, feathers or hair,
    Haunting stream, standing-pool, cockloft or common,
    From their mud, hole or perch, kennel or lair.

    Take these two newspapers, wet with men's
    water ——

Anic. Of my girl's making, nevertheless.

    Salt. Mind not the ancient dame; envy has taught
    her ——·

Anic. Knowledge of earthenware, rather confess.

Salt. Clap them upon your head, occiput, sinciput —

Anic. But do it tenderly, else they will tear.

Sus. They 're your own daily sheets.   Mind not the stingy slut.

Salt. Press them to mouth and nose, eyelids and hair.

Dead. But they are devilish salt.
Salt. That 's not the devil's fault.
Fledg. No, 't is humanity's.
     Anic. That you may swear.

Salt. As in the *Hours'* page flatness and fickleness,
  Laughable graveness and mawkish mirth meet;
  As in the *Cryer* mere spluttering words express
  All that 's not ribald or worse in its sheet;

  So shall these papers impress on your faces
  Types of each soul's inward birth-given shape,
  Make Deadhead a parrot, give you the grimaces,
  The solemn inaneness and mirth of an ape.

It is done.   Lift the sheet;
The impression 's complete.

Dead. I am glad; for the print 's too much stal'd to be sweet.

Anic. Eh, the trio! How fine!

Sus. But my asshead 's the best.

Anic. And I alone left, all unchang'd!

                      Sus. Don't be vex'd.

Anic. When my virtue alone in the group 's unexpress'd?

I were better unsex'd.

Salt. You need not repine:

You attract as much note

By your petticoat.

Fledg. And are free of the brine.

Dead. A parrot, a monkey, an ass and old maid.

Let us get up a dance for our masquerade.

Fledg. But where is the music?

                  Salt. Behold, to your aid.

Fledg. The fiddle, the bones and the banjo already!

I fear that the Devil is piper.

                  Salt. Not he.

Sus. They come from the spirits.

                  Salt. No matter; keep steady:

You *may* have the Devil to pay, but not me.

Sus. That is something; I like contributions post-free.

Fledg. But, Doctor, turn in.

                Sus. I am fagg'd. Ere you came,

I danc'd a long Indian pas-seul for my fame,

And toe'd it unbreech'd, proof to cold and to shame.

Dead. Then you 've practice; a male Taglioni. Fall in.

Scrape up now, good catgut, and let us begin.

Fledg. Up and down, and in and out,
    Chassez, promenez round about.
Dead. It is better leg-shaking, than pens, no doubt.
    Fol de rol !

Sus. The one is hard shuffling, the other mere play.
    No donkey could stand that, except for pay.
Fledg. You mean, I suppose, for thistles or hay.
Sus. It is one.   And an ass cannot always bray
    Without pause in his vocalization.

Dead. And a parrot must swing, as well as talk.
Fledg. And a monkey won't always on two legs walk.
Anic. Nor a petticoat either swap cheese for chalk,
    Who is not in a situation.
Sus. Except ——
    Dead. But, Doctor, keep time ; you balk.
Sus. — For a handsome consid-e-ration.
Dead. Fol de rol.

Fledg. Cross over.   Ladies change.   You see,
    We beat the devils in *Calvary.*
Dead. That is easy ; they danc'd without fiddle-de-dee
    Fol de lol.

Fledg. Balance.   I never had so much fun,
    Except when I found an author done.
Dead. Or the public diddled.
                Anic. It is all one,

In our soi-disant critical function.

Fledg. To cog, dissemble, misrepresent;
　　To fool the public to its bent;
　　And wink when it sees what never was meant;
　　Is interest rich; but cent per cent ——
Sus. Is our Terpsichorean junction.

Dead. Forward two.　What a jolly dance!
Fledg. And what music!　'T would make an old donkey
　　　　prance.
Sus. Or a tailless monkey.
　　　　　　Fledg. Its pleasures enhance,
　　And with a particular zest,
　　The joy I had to make Tilton cry,
　　When I quoted as proof of his powers *The Fly.*
Dead. Well, why did n't Sheldon your blarney buy?
Fledg. Or yours?　You know, as well as I,
　　He may rank with New England's best.[25]

Dead. One jackass foward.　Now back again.
　　Now lady and ape.
　　　　　　Anic. Let me hold up my train.
Dead. Come, Be'lzebub, scrape us another strain.
　　Fol de lol.

　　　　Enter GALANTUOM, HEARTANDHEAD,
　　　　　　and ATTICUS.

Gal. Why, what the deuse are you all about?

Sus. Do you see our heads?

              Gal. To be sure we do.

And your legs as well.   You 're a jolly crew.

Few editors, even the dolts of *the Nation*,

Would after this fashion make saltation

To fiddle and flute.   You caper without.

Sus. You must be stone-deaf and gravel-blind.

Don't you see our little band ?

'T is of the best of the fiddling kind

To be found 'in all the land.

Saltpeter has now the horsehair in hand,

And Brimstone rattles the bones,

And little Charcoal'

From the banjo's hole

Is drawing those bullfrog tones.

Gal. The devil ! the banjo has no hole.

Heart. He must mean " the light guitar."

Sus. No, I don't; I mean just what I say :

The banjo's bottom is all away.

Dead. And as Sambo says, *dat 's dar.* —

No matter, strike up,

My devils-bullpup,

And show them what you are.

    Fledg. Up the middle and down again.

    Dead. Sweep in, broomsticks, might and main.

    Sus. Rest for muscle is rust for brain.

    Anic. Up the middle and down again.

Att. Why, they are all four crazy!

       Fledg. Are we so?

You are, all three, fools.

Dead. You are blind as new kittens, and don't seem to know
 There 's lots of pleasure in such a go.

Sus. " Dul'ce est desip'ere in loco'."

Anic. What is that?

Dead. Some Hebrew that 's pat,
 Fundamentally taught in the schools.

Sus. But you don't mark my ears' length, you don't note my
   head,
 Those emblems of glory to be.
 Be abash'd when you learn there lurks under this shed
 The brain of Sus, double L. D.
 Behold too that green-noddled parrot, that monkey
 Which belongs to the kind that are minus a tail:
 The first one picks grubs from the *Cryer* man's nail,
 The other is turnspit to Weathercock Flunky.

Heart. A parrot, a monkey, a head and long ears!
 This is worse than the Quarterly gabble of Sears.

Fledg. And you see not the changes?

       Gal. We see but three men,
 Two of whom have their faces
 Smear'd with what seems the traces
 Of types, and an elderly dame, in this den.

Sus. And you heard not the music?

       Att. We heard upon the floor
 The shuffling of your feet and your bacchanalian roar,
 As you shambled to and fro.

Only this.

 Dead. Says Raven Poe :

" Only this, and nothing more."

Sus. And you don't then see the triad ?

      Att. What triad ?

       Sus. Our small band,

With the banjo, and the beef-bones, and the fiddle-bow in
 hand.

There they stand.

Att. Where ?

   Sus. At the wall.

Att. I see but a petticoat ——

     Dead. " Hanging to dry." [26]

Att. And an old straw bonnet by,

 And a shawl.

Sus. Then you 're crazy, else am I.

Att. To my thinking,

 It is wine.

Fledg. What the Doctor has been drinking,

 With the ancient virgin here,

 Is his own affair.

 But, I say it without shrinking,

 Save our-beer,

 Dead and I have tasted nothing ——

      Dead. Only brine.

Fledg. Yet we see the ass's ear,

 And behold the triad there,

 Who have, to our delectation,

 Made this triple transformation.

That is clear.

Gal. Here 's some juggle.

        Sus. You are crazy.

Mr. Peter, Charcoal, Brim:

Lift these skeptics' leaden eyes.

In this room the air 's not hazy,

No more burns the candle dim;

In the gaslight ——

        Dead. Even an ass might

At your blindness show surprise.

Salt. As I hinted once before,

    Strangers to your worth are blind;

    And the glory of your asshood ·

    With your friends alone will pass good,

    Monkies, parrots, and such kind.

    This, although 't you may deplore, —

Dead. " Quoth the Raven, Evermore," —

Salt. 'T is not in our power to alter.

    Only human optics heed us

    In the sconce of fools who need us,

    Who with truth and conscience palter

    Or are like yourself in mind.

Sus. Did you hear ?

        Gal. What ? Deadhead's joke ?

Sus. No, that other voice which spoke.

Gal. No one else the stillness broke.

Att. We were struck to see you staring

    At those rags for women's wearing,

    As if pondering their repairing,

Hanging on the dingy wall.

Sus. Then the devil must be in it!

O my asshead! And to win it,

Was 't for this I stoop'd to shin it?

Bore with kick and spank and thwack?

More, bore Charcoal on my back?

Nor that all;

Swung like smok'd meat from the ceiling,

Stood on end till brains were reeling,

And, my southern pole revealing,

Boldly let my breeches fall?

Dead. So the game is up! We 're diddled.

'T was old Be'lzebub that fiddled.

Let 's *skedaddle*, great and small.

Salt. But before you scud, believe me,

In this mummery goëtic

There was nothing to deceive ye.

Each shall flourish still a critic,

With the traits that here he bore.

You shall be, to all who know you,

Still a parrot, and a monkey,

Mimicking and nothing more,

He who turns the spit for Flunky.

Still the ancient dame shall drape her

In old frippery and shape her

Worn head-gear to suit her paper;

While the LL.D. shall show you

All his asshead as before.

Heart. How they stare! They are surely crazy.

Dead. No, we 're listening but; be aisy.

Sus. To a prophecy, expressing ——

Fledg. That our cake is not all dough.

Salt. Take, before you leave, this blessing.

Brim. Mine too.

   Char. Mine too, Doctor.

     Sus. Oh!

Spare! Have mercy! Such a basting

For my ham is more than wasting:

I 've no relish for the dressing. [*Exit — manipulating.*

Gal. Good night, Doctor.

   Dead. There 's a go!

Take more time. With so much hasting,

You may reach too soon below.

Fledg. Come, old fellows, not for us

Such rump-roasting.

   Dead. Don't stay tasting:

Let us hasten after Sus.

Fledg. D—n them, no; pitch in.

   Dead. Our breeches

'Gainst their hoofs have slim defences.

Damn'd they are. Come, St. Paul teaches

Counter-kicking never thrives.

Sus. [*from below.*] Bring down with you, lads, my beaver. —

Take my curse, you arch deceiver!

Salt. Why? Your asshood aye survives.

Att. Have these men not lost their senses?

Heart. Were they ever theirs, to lose them?

Gal. Look! you 'd think their legs had lives.

Dead. Gad! we 've no choice but to use them.
Needs must when the devil drives.

Exeunt hastily
FLEDGLING *and* DEADHEAD,
*the former in tragic huff, and are followed
deliberately and wonderingly by*
GALANTUOM, HEARTANDHEAD *and* ATTICUS.

SALTPETER, BRIMSTONE, *and* CHARCOAL,
first lifting up ANICULA *by the petticoat, causing her to
sprawl and kick out like a toy spider, to the great damage of her
virginal modesty, convert the medical advertisements of the*
Hours *and the* Cryer *into sulphuretted hydrogen
and ascend through the ceiling by the vapor.*

Manet
ANICULA *in dishabille,*
with the blank expression of the Ethnos.

21*

NOTES

THE SCHOOL FOR CRITICS

1.—P. 405. — *Slanghouse-Square* —] There is a place in New-York with a somewhat similar composite name, borrowed in like manner, with a ridiculous apery, from a locality in London. But in that case it is a triangle, a scalene of the most irregular proportions, and indeed amorphous, the two longest sides not meeting at all, although they converge. However, a figure of three angles for a parallelogram is as near as the journal which originated the euphonious designation can be expected to come to correctness.

2.—P. 405. — *in rogues abounding, Who draw from the public pot their fare And openly*, etc.] This is so like the kind of men which Mr. Parton gave to public admiration in the *N. American Review*, that, were it not for the name of the city, one might suppose they sat for the outline in New York. But as no individual is whatever his pre-eminence, absolutely singular, so it may be that every corporation has, however monstrous its rascality, somewhere its congeners.

3.—P. 406. *That is why, one day, To get appointed*, etc.] This is one of the bad features of our popular government, the nomination to high office of members of the Press. Supposing they were equally well-qualified as certain others, — which is taking a very great deal on assumption, — yet the office serves as a bribe, and the influence of a widely circulating newspaper is cheaply bought at any price by the candidate for election or re-election to the Presidency. The corruption thus produced on both sides, in the relation of cause and effect, needs not to be demoustrated.

4.—P. 408. *And stirring up rubbish he cry'd, " Oh fine ! "*] It was not to be expected that any professional critic would presume to attack an author of established reputation, far less that those who know nothing of literary criticism but its pretension should be able to discriminate between the false and the true ; but that such an exhibition of absurdity should be made in any journal of standing as is paraded, with full trumpet-accompaniment, in the following passage of the *N. Y. Times* of May 18, 1867, would be incredible except to those familiar with its sycophancy in letters, or who know by experience its ignorance therein and absolute indifference to principle.

"Sometimes too, it would seem that Mr. Longfellow's exceeding familiarity with the Italian, and his unswerving attention to its literal signification leads [lead] him into obscurity. An instance of this may be found in the sixth line of canto XXIV. which Mr. Longfellow renders —

' But little lasts the temper of her pen.'

The word pen here is precisely the same as the original *penna*, but the reader who knows nothing of DANTE would be in doubt as to the meaning of the line. So in line thirty-six of the same canto :

' He I know not, but I had been dead beat.'

The last half of this line has never been equaled by any former translator."

I should think not. It is a "dead beat" altogether. Had I, or Cluvienus, used such slang — on any occasion whatever ! And for so ordinary a phrase :

"Non so di lui ; ma lo sarei *ben vinto*."

The fact is, if the specimens given in the *Times* and in the *Tribune* are fair examples of Mr. Longfellow's work, it will show that his capacity as a poet is, in every respect, far below what even his most moderate admirers have allowed him. Mr. L., it may be supposed, considered, that, as Dante himself frequently uses coarse and even grotesque phrases, he was but imitating the Dantescan spirit when he introduced this vulgarism and slang of the turf or chase. If so, he transcended his part, which was to follow, not to lead, and not to libel his original by adding to his crudities. But these newspaper critics! * ——

* The *Times* goes on to cite what it calls an "incomparable picture:"

> " Quivi sospiri, pianti ed alti guai
> Risonavan per l'aer senza stelle,
> Perch' io al cominciar ne lagrimai.
>   Diverse lingue, orribili favelle,
> Parole di dolore, accenti d'ira,
> Voci alte e fioche, e suon di man con elle,
>   Facevano un tumulto il qual s'aggira
> Sempre 'n quell' aria senza tempo tinta,
>   Come la rena quando 'l turbo spira." (*Inf.* III.)

Of this it gives seven translations. The best of these is, as might be supposed, the German; but "of all the English versions," it tells us, — in the face of Mr. Wright's and Dr. Parsons', — "Mr. Longfellow's is unquestionably both the most literal and the most *poetic*." . . . Let us have it, including the two extraordinary lines here italicized :

> "There sighs, complaints and ululations loud
>   Resounded through the air without a star.
>   Whence I, at the beginning, wept thereat.
> *Languages diverse, horrible dialects,*
>   *Accents of anger, words of agony*
> And voices high and hoarse, with sound of hands,
>   Made up a tumult that goes whirling on
> Forever in that air forever black
> Even as the sand doth when the whirlwind breathes."

I knew beforehand, judging from such as I have redd of Mr. Longfellow's poems, and redd (the smaller ones) with unqualified admiration, that their author was by the very character of his mind inadequate to a version of the stern and masculine Florentine, but I never could have dreamed that he would have the folly to attempt, in these days, to render him without the rhyme which is so es-

5.—P. 410. *Amen! as said on his knees Jeff Davis*, etc.] Godliness was a characteristic trait of this eminent personage, — eminent, I mean, in virtues. A lady of Richmond was much edified by seeing

sential to a true imitation. But my greatest surprise has been at the translator's blank verse. His extraordinary use of unaccented syllables, where, at the close of a line, an accented one is required (whether that be the final syllable itself, or with other syllables after it redundant), shows a singular want of comprehension of true rythm and a defect of ear that I can scarcely now account for, although it is not an uncommon occurrence where poets used to rhyme attempt to do without it. In fine, his version (if it may be estimated by the samples given by his eulogists) is not even respectable, and, from a man of his taste, is, in a bad sense, surprising. Yet in the passage above quoted, which the newspaper-man, with affected transport, calls "superb", telling us that *its marvelous words thrill over every nerve of the reader !* (ª) there is nothing difficult at all, either of comprehension or of rendering.

Having, in *Arthur Carryl*, given a translation of certain scraps there cited of Dante, and given them, according to my constant custom, in the measure of the original, and with corresponding or equivalent rhymes, years before Mr. L. attempted his version, I hope I have some right to put forward my own rendering of the place, not to show how well it may be done, but to show that it may be done, and easily too, better than he has done it. These are the lines, written after running over the absurd and pedantic panegyric I have, for my readers' sake as well as for my own, held up to ridicule, and the contempt which befits at all times the hypocrisy of literary dilletanteism.

> There sighs, laments, and howlings of deep woo,
> Resounded through that air without a star.
> Wherefore, at first, my tears could not but flow.
>
> Tongues of all kinds, and horrible words that jar,
> Phrases of suffering, wrath's discordant sound,
> Shrieks and chok'd cries, and smitten hands, that for
> And near made tumult, to and fro rebound,
> Forever in that air's unchanging gloom,
> Like to the sand which eddying winds whirl round.

I do not aver that this exactitude of imitation could be carried out (even with

(ª) There is nothing whatever "marvelous" in either words or verse, although there is much that is admirable in both. This is the pitiful cant of would-be connoisseurs, who before any work of art, from letters to music, affect a rapture proportioned to its celebrity, and endeavor, by guessing at the value of certain points, or by assuming it without guessing, to acquire the reputation of literary acumen. As for Mr. L.'s translation, it is obvious to any unbiassed reader, and certainly to one who has true knowledge of the subject and of verse in general, that three of the lines are the merest prose, while it is a desecration of the song of the Tuscan to render his accurate rythm by the absolutely unmetrical line which is the middle as well as worst of these three :

" *Languages diverse, horrible dialects*."

him, through his open window, on his Presidential knees, and took care to advertise it to the public. To shut himself in his closet and pray in secret, according to the precept of Christ, would have been putting his rushlight under a bushel and have deprived the God-devoted of the profit of its lustre. What a sacrifice even of modesty will men not make, when exalted above self by the vapor of an ebullient patriotism!

It was perhaps for his sanctity that this intended martyr, who had had the self-denial to run from destiny in his wife's petticoat, was recently cheered on 'Change in Liverpool. It was certainly not because he recommended his State to dishonor its own bonds, nor because he endorsed for consideration the proposition to murder Lincoln, nor that he claimed to make the cornerstone of his temple of human rights the absolute negation of human liberty, that our cousins of England forgot they had just found out how much they loved us.

6.—P. 414. *No, none of us are so squeamous.*] It is probably, not from habitual vulgarity, but from love of antiquity and his familiarity with old English writers, that the *Cryer's* man uses this, now unjustly considered barbarous and corrupt, form of the word "squeamish." Webster, whom I have so often occasion to find fault with, has absurdly the hypothesis, "Probably from the root of *wamble.*" Chaucer wrote *squaimous ;* and his erudite editor tells us: "Robert of Brunne (in his translation of *Manuel des Pechées*, Ms. Bod. 2078. fol. 46.) writes this word, *esquaimous ;* which is nearer to its original, *exquamiare*, a corruption of *excambiare.*" TYRWHITT: Gloss. Chauc. *ad v.* In *Rich. Cœr de L.* (ed. Weber,) it is written *squoymous :* "Frendes, be not squoymous, etc.," when the Saracens have the heads of their friends placed in the dishes before them. This is precisely, in its signification, the modern *squeamish.*

single rhyme as here) through the whole of the *Commedia*, but I am positive that without such imitation, though one may give the measure of the poet, he cannot render his *tone*, which is to his stanzas what the coloring is to a fine painting in which that quality is prominent.

7.—P. 420. *You have lost, sir and ma'am, each the nice speciality,* etc.] Fledgling is, like most imperfectly educated persons who are literary pretenders, not always to be held responsible for verbal innovations; but, in the present instance, he is not so far out of the way, this form of the substantive — *speciality* for *specialty* — though not used, being in perfect analogy with that of the words it rhymes with in the text. Besides, it is correcter etymologically, the term having come in to us from the French, *spécialité,* used in the same sense.

P.S. Since the note was written, I have found the word in the form 'speciality' in a philosophical treatise of the present day; in Dr. David Page's Essay on "Man," p. 153, N. Y. ed. 1868, — unless it is there a misprint.

8.—P. 422. *What a phrase is that!*] See above, note 4.

For the allusion to Fernando, there is in a cognate Review of similar pretensions to those of Dr. Sus's, a passage which will perhaps explain it. As a few years hence men might grope in vain for its fossilized existence, I shall go to the expense of printing the article entire, and with all its curiosities of word, syllable and point, as I find them on pp. 415–417 of the XIVth vol. of *The National Quarterly Review, Edited by Edward I. Sears, A.M., LL.D.* — The footnotes are made to supply what the Doctor in his "friendly and benevolent spirit" constrained himself to suppress.

"*Calvary — Virginina.   Tragedies.* By LAUGHTON OSBORN. 12mo., pp. 200. New York: Doolady. 1857.

"In general Mr. Doolady exhibits considerable judgment in his selections; it is but seldom that we have had any serious fault to find with his publications. Nor does the one now before us form an exception; although we do not think that Laughton Osborn will ever occupy a high rank among tragic writers. He may succeed in other departments of literature, but we can assure him in all kindness that tragedy is not his forte; nor is poetry in any form. After making full allowance for the disadvantage under which he has labored in treating the subjects he has chosen, we see nothing to justify us in the opinion that he would have succeeded under more favorable circumstances.

"The incidents which he has attempted to dramatise in 'Calvary' are at once too familiar and too mysterious. Even Milton has failed in his 'Paradise Regained.' The life and death of Christ are so fully detailed in the New Testament that it would require a genius of a high order to invest the subject with that air of novelty which is essential to the drama. This is admirably illustrated in the *Divina Commedia* of Dante, although not a drama in the strict sense of the term. There is no intelligent person who has read that truly sublime poem who has not observed a vast difference between the *Purgatorio* and the *Paradiso*; but a still greater difference between the *Inferno* and the *Paradiso*, the latter being greatly inferior to either of the former.

"The reason is obvious enough; while neither sacred nor profane history has much to say on what passes in purgatory or hell, each is quite copious on what relates to paradise considered as the happiness derived by man from the death of Christ.

"If however, it be urged that paradise is not familiar, being *extra terram*, the same claim cannot be made for Calvary. That the events which took place at Calvary were in the highest degree tragic is beyond dispute; but, as already observed, all the incidents and circumstances that led to it are so fully described that but little room is left for the exercise of the fancy. Were it otherwise, we think there would still be some objection to the exhibition of Jesus, the Archangels, Mary, the mother of Jesus, Mary Magdalene Simon Peter, &c., on the stage, at least in the style in which it is done in Laughton Osborn's 'Calvary.' *

"Milton was content to commence his Paradise Lost with what took place on our own sphere — 'man's first disobedience,' &c. Homer soared no higher at the outset than the wrath of Achilles. Nor has Virgil attempted a different course. But our present author lays his first scene in heaven, and his first speakers are Raphael and Michael, who have a chorus of angels, though, in sooth, rather a discordant one. In Scene III. Jesus, Mary and Martha appear, the *locus* being 'A room in the dwelling of Jesus' Mother.' If the dialogue which takes place between the Saviour of mankind and his Mother had been intended for a burlesque it could hardly have seemed to us more profane. But we cheerfully do the author the justice to believe that he means well throughout. Mary addresses Jesus, 'O my darling!' and tells him that what He says is to happen

---

* If the reader should think it incredible that the fool, who wrote this stuff, actually supposed that a drama like *Calvary* (even if such was the author's intention) could, with its angels and devils, its scenes in Heaven and in Hell, and the act of the crucifixion, be put upon the stage, in any style, I can only tell him that I copy literally, and I did not make the fellow's brains.

makes her 'blood curdle'.* In another part of the same dialogue she is made
to say :

> ' I am thy mother, Jesus, and my heart
> Warms to thee now as when I first beheld thee
> After my weary travail,' &c. — (p. 9.) †

"When Martha enters Mary appeals to her, as if she had more influence on
Jesus than herself, thus :

> ' Kneel with me, Martha ! *He has love for thee.*
> Tell him he kills me ! Tell him ! ——' ‡

"The first scene of the second act is laid in hell, and the interlocutors are
Lucifer and Beelzebub, who have a chorus of evil spirits which differs very
slightly, if anything, from the chorus of angels, except that the former is, perhaps, a little more lugubrious than the latter. Next come Judas Iscariot and
Mary Magdalene. Judas speaks quite idiomatically. 'Ugh !' he says, 'and the

---

* *Mary.* And canst thou speak with calmness, when my heart
Is aching for thee ? Jesus, O my son !
Think on thy mother, and avoid the storm
That now is darkening o'er thee, and whose shadow
Makes my blood curdle with the chill of death.
For my sake, O my darling !

† *Mary.* Stay yet a little. By that happy time
Thou hast thyself remember'd, when these breasts
That now are wither'd fed thee from my blood,
I do adjure thee ! Thou hast call'd me Mother
With that sweet voice, although again the tone
That is so stern and lofty, when thou speak'st
Those riddles that I dare not try to solve,
Has aw'd and check'd me, — thou hast call'd me Mother.
I am thy mother, Jesus, and my heart
Warms to thee now as when I first beheld thee
After my weary travail ; see me now
Embrace thy feet, and pray thee as my god,
For my sake, for thy own ! ——

‡ *Jesus.* Thou hast spoken, Martha, loyally and well.
But, in that faith and wisdom, seest thou not
That I should need no warning ? Even now
The heart that shall betray me is convuls'd
With its distracting passions, and the hand
Is itching for the silver that shall buy
My body for the cross. It is decreed.
Mary. Mean'st thou this fully ? Canst thou still so calmly
Speak what to credit is —— My son ! my son !
Kneel with me, Martha ! He has love for thee.
Tell him he kills me ! Tell him ! —— Jesus, son !
Have mercy on me ! Save thyself — and me !

lamp looks dying.' She replies: 'Be not displeas'd, dear Judas.' (p. 15.) Fur
ther on in the same dialogue she addresses him:

> 'That starv'd look worries me; and, oh! the chill
> Of this unwholesome lodging!' — (p. 15.) *

"We have not yet got beyond the second act; and the tragedy extends
to five acts, occupying seventy-four pages. Under these circumstances we
think our readers will excuse us if we cannot proceed any farther in this direction.

"*Virginina* is a better effort than 'Calvary', but we are very much afraid that
it will not succeed as a tragedy. The Romans, male and female, are made to express themselves considerably more like New Yorkers than is in strict accordance
with the truth of history. The following is a pretty favorable specimen:

> *Icil.* — 'I am Icilius, and should the people
> The sole legitimate source of sovereign rule,
> For that they are the many, and their thews
> Strain to heave up, to prop and keep sustain'd
> The edifice whose chambers ye but fill.' — (p. 108.)

"Fernando Wood could hardly have expressed himself more democratically or

---

> * *Judas.* The night is chilly. Hast thou not a coal
> To feed the brazier? Not one drop of wine?
> Ugh! and the lamp looks dying. Where is gone
> The shekel that I gave thee yesternight?
> *Magd.* Be not displeas'd, dear Judas. I bestow'd it
> But as the Master seem'd to say we ought:
> I cast it in the Treasury.
>   *Judas.* Like that widow
> Whose paltry mites he made of more account
> Than all the rest, because they were her all.
> So thou must give thy all! Of many fools
> Of Magdala, thou, Mary, art the best.
> Why not have gone at once to the perfumer's,
> Like thy Bethanian namesake, and anoint
> His yellow locks, or even smear his feet,
> As I have seen thee sweep them oftentimes
> With these long delicate hairs (I could defile them!)
> He would have thought still more of it.
>   *Magd.* For shame!
> Thou speakest of our Lord, the Christ, our King.
> *Judas.* I know not that: I know that I am weary
> Of waiting for his kingdom, which I thought
> Would make us rich at least, — both thee and me.
> That starv'd look worries me: and oh, the chill
> Of this unwholesome lodging! With that shekel
> Thou might'st have bought us fire and light and food.

more patriotically than this when a candidate for Governor of the State.* We cheerfully admit, however, that there are some good passages in Virginina, but we hope we shall be excused if we prefer to let the reader discover them for himself.

"Before we conclude we beg to give the author one word of advice, which we trust he will accept in the same friendly, benevolent spirit in which it is offered. He announces to us on one of the fly-leaves of this volume that the two pieces we have just glanced at 'are the first of a series of *nineteen*, which, with the exception of two, are now completed and ready for the press.' This is followed by the titles of ten tragedies and seven comedies! We have no doubt that Mr. Osborn is as much at home in comedy as he is in tragedy; nay, we think he is more successful in exciting laughter even when he does not mean to do so, than he is in drawing forth tears when most tragically inclined. At the same time, we would advise him to withhold his 'Silver Head' and 'Double Deceit' (comedies) until the peo-

---

* *Icil.* I am Icilius, and I hold the people
    The sole legitimate source of sovereign rule,
    For that they are the many, and their thews
    Strain to heave up, to prop and keep sustain'd,
    The edifice whose chambers ye but fill.
    Were Appius not your master as our tyrant,
    My hate to your cruel order were not less,
    And, the decemvirate overthrown, Icilius
    Steps on its carcase, to do battle still
    For freedom and the people's rights.   Thou hearest; —
    These are my motives.   What are thine?
                        Lucr. I am
    Lucretius, and the common folk of Rome
    I have in hatred less than in disdain.
    But is there eye so blear'd that sees not Appius
    Striding to sovereign rule across our necks?
    He cring'd to the people, and they set him o'er them.
    He trod them down.   He cringes now to us.
    And Rome beholds the guardians of her state
    Become mere servitors to the usurping Ten,
    Whose plural tyranny even now is merging
    Into the singular rule of this bold man.
    I love my order, and will let no Tarquin
    Level its pillars to rear himself a throne.
    These are my motives.
                    Icil. And they please me little;
    As does thy purpled tunic, which they suit.
    But thou dost much; for thou 'rt a man; thy tongue
    Fears not to utter what thy soul dares think.

Thus, the language of Icilius, *which is considerably more like that of a New-Yorker than is strictly accordant with the truth of history*, is addressed to one of the proudest of the patricians, and not, as the truthful reviewer would advise us, to the class of people *Fernando Wood harangues when a candidate for the State Governorship*. The misrepresentation however is not greater than that in every other part of the "notice," beginning with "*Virginina*"; but it is probably less intentional, as being the result of stupidity as well as of envy and malevolence.

ple are much more predisposed to laughter than they are at present, and have more time and money to spare."

And such is the critical record of such a poem as *Virginia!* What will the men of the future think of our standing as a cultivated people, and of the literary judgment and the fair-dealing of our critics, when they are told that this flippant, pedantic, ill-digested and badly-written school-exercise, with its low-bred impertinence, its thinly-vailed and hypocritical maliguity, and its brazen-faced falsehood, is the sole notice that has been taken of that tragedy in all the number of our Quarterly Reviews?

9.—P. 423. *Which in all countries, as late I said,* etc., etc.] I fear I have been led into plagiarism; for these identical phrases occur in a work of prodigiously high standing.

"It is almost superfluous to remark," says the author of a review of *Alfieri's Life and Writings,* in the XIVth vol. *N. Y. Nat. Rev.* p. 216, "that Alfieri was not entitled to the degree of Master to which he thus refers; but degrees have been conferred in all countries and ages in which there are colleges and universities under similar circumstances; they are conferred at the present day."

It is true, there is scarcely anything but misrepresentation in the whole article, and its literary judgments are only a little worse than its travesty of Alfieri's Italian; but, for the remark about the manner in which degrees are given, we, looking on the cover of the journal, where we read *A.M.,* write "Approved."

10.—P. 423. *In Heidelberg . . . . . A British noble got LL.D. Conferr'd on his horse.*] I had this story on the Neckar, from an Oxford student on his vacation tour. He gave it as an illustration of the freedom with which the German University dispensed its favors. The nobleman handed-in the name of his Bucephalus, and nothing further was asked.

11.—P. 423. *A letter'd ass* — "*haud absurdum est.*" '*T is* facere *well reïpublicæ.*] By a strange coincidence, there is a motto on one of our Reviews, "Pulchrum est bene facere reipublicæ, etiam *bene dicere* haud absurdum est." Some may think it should read *male-dicere.* As Sus says in the text, the words serve to keep his brain-pan soft; and they may be as efficacious in a title-page.

12.—P. 428. *Because Alger in his* Solitude, *etc.*]

" 'The penalty,' says the author, 'affixed to supremely equipped souls is that they must often be left alone on the cloudy eminence of their greatness, amid the lightnings, the stars, and the canopy, commanding the sovereign prospects indeed, but sighing for the warm breath of the vale, and the friendly embraces of men.' . . To come down from the canopy, we should be very glad to know what all this sighing and gnashing of teeth is about. * * Byron without his mask was a very ordinary sort of person. * * It is indisputable that he liked women ["God help the wicked!"], especially if they were the wives of other men, and the poor heart-broken poet saw a chance to destroy the happiness and blacken the good fame of a quiet household [!]. He pretended to cling to an early attachment, but if he had married the young lady [which?] it is more than probable that he would have treated her as badly, as wickedly, as brutally as he actually treated the lady whose life was cursed by her union with him. The real extent of the baseness of his conduct toward Lady Byron will never be known now, but the one or two who did know of it [know it] declare that it was monstrous beyond conception [! !]. It was no woman's jealousy or pique which darkened poor Lady Byron's days. Those who remember the hints thrown out in a narrative of her life which appeared a few years ago in the London *Daily News* [therefore perfectly reliable] will not need to be informed that the melancholy poet was capable of the vilest acts. He had many less culpable faults [than these "vilest acts" presumed from "hints"]. He liked pleasure [naughty fellow!]. He drank, he gambled, he was consumed with vanity [and drank to cool himself], he had intrigues with men's [not boys'] wives and boasted of them, he turned round and abused his dupes in his poetry for being false to their husbands [eh?], he lied habitually, and he was mean and cunning [all of which propensities, acts, and habits, form what are so curiously called *less culpable faults*]." *N. Y. Times,* Thursday, May 2, 1867.

Alger did indeed talk like a fool, if his style is as above quoted; but this is to grunt and growl like a beast.

13.—P. 428. *And Emerson's verse without rhyming close, And a devilish deal less tough.*]

" The longest poem in the present collection is entitled 'May-Day'. . . . . It *breathes* throughout the freshness and the beauty of Spring, and *overflows* with poetic thought and imaginative *sympathy with the breaking of the 'marble sleep'* of Winter. [Good lack-a-day ! where is Alger ?] . . . What a- graphic piece of description is this :

> Lo ! how all the tribes combine
> To rout the flying foe.
> See, every *patriot* oak-leaf throws
> His elfin length upon the snows ;
> Not idle, since the leaf all day
> Draws to the spot the solar ray,
> Ere sunset quarrying inches down,
> And half-way to the mosses brown :
> While the grass beneath the rime
> Has hints of the propitious time,
> And upward pries and perforates
> Through the cold slab a thousand gates,
> Till green lances peering through
> Bend happy in the welkin blue." *N. Y. Times*, May 1, 1867.

The *grass having hints, and prying and perforating in a slab a thousand gates*, and *lances peering* and *bending happy*, is so good that we will cut off this quotation here. Then :

" The northward procession of the Spring is thus vividly described :

> I saw the bud-crowned Spring go forth,
> Stepping daily onward north
> To greet staid ancient *cavaliers*
> Filing single in stately train.
> And who, and who *are* the *travelers !*
> They *were* Night and Day, and Day and Night,
> Pilgrims wight *with step forthright.*
> I saw the Days deformed and *low,*
> *Short* and bent by cold and snow ;
> The merry Spring threw wreaths on them,
> [Which was a *mauvaise plaisanterie*, as they were already snow-bowed]
> Flower-wreaths gay with bud and bell ;
> Many a flower and many a gem,
> *They were refreshed by the smell.*
> They shook the snow from hats and shoon,
> They put their April raiment on ;
> *And those eternal forms* ["deformed and low"]

> *Unhurt by a thousand storms*
> [Yet bent by the weight of snow]
> *Shot up to the height of the sky again,*
> And danced as merrily as young men."

Fancy them, these *pilgrims wight with step forthright, shooting up to the height of the sky, then dancing away right merrily :* The image is of Longinistic sublimity, and one is tempted to ask with the big-worded Grecian, *Where the devil did they find the space?* But let us continue : it is such a treat to have a pretentious and affected philosopher writing — well, such verses as a child should be spanked for.

> " I saw them mask their awful glance
> *Sidewise meek in gossamer lids ;*
> And to speak my thought if none forbids,
> It was as if *the eternal gods,*
> *Tired of their starry periods,* [acc. *periods'*]
> Hid their majesty in cloth
> *Woven of tulips and painted moth.*
> On carpets green the *maskers* marc'd
> Below May's well-appointed arch,
> *Each star, each god, each grace artain,*

[all made out of the *pilgrims wight,* who, vailing *their awful glance's* light, *Sidewise meek, if* no sense *forbids, in gossamer lids, maskers* grow in a Joseph's cloth *Woven of tulips and painted moth.* — By the by, as moths do not come out in April, with paint or without, nor the tulips either I believe, where did the *cavalier-traveler-Days* deformed get their wardrobe *Unhurt by a thousand storms* for their eternal sky-high *forms?*]

> Every joy and *virtue speed,* [?]
> Marching duly in her train,
> And *fainting* Nature at her need
> Is made *whole* again."
> [It 's a wonder she was not driven stark-mad.]

And the fool or sycophant praises this stuff of Emerson's, who, besides having his head half-way up in a Swinburne fog, and being almost as incapable of rythm as Walt Whitman, has no adequate conception of what is rhyme !

> " We give space to one extract more, the closing passage of the poem.
>
> > For thou, O Spring ! canst renovate
> > All that high God did first create.

> Be still his *arm and architect,*
> Rebuild the ruin, mend defect;
> *Chemist* to *vamp* old worlds with new,
> *Coat sea* and sky with heavenlier blue,
> New-tint the plumage of the birds,
> And *slough decay* from grazing herds, etc."

We shall follow no further. The image of the *chemist* turned cobbler and *vamping old worlds with new,* though he does not tell how the feat is done, which were a considerable one even were it *old shoes with new,* and the *sloughing of decay* from cattle while grazing (an excellent thing in the present panic of the meat-market,) make too delectable an ending for us to mar it by addition.

14. —P. 428. *As pompous an ass as Victor Hugo,* Who, etc., etc.] One of the best-marked personal traits of this greatly overrated poet and romancer, is conspicuous in the following note taken from the *N. Y. Times* of July 30, 1867.

"Letter from Victor Hugo on John Brown.
From la Coöpération.
The editor of this journal, having opened a subscription with a view to offering a medal to JOHN BROWN'S widow, received the subjoined letter from VICTOR HUGO:

Hauteville House, July 3, 1867.
Sir: My name belongs to all who would make use of it to serve progress and truth.
A medal to LINCOLN calls for a medal to JOHN BROWN. Let us cancel that debt pending such time as AMERICA shall cancel hers. America owes JOHN BROWN a statue as tall as that of WASHINGTON. WASHINGTON 'founded' America, JOHN BROWN diffused liberty.
I press your hand.
VICTOR HUGO."

Here wo see lack of judgment in the exaltation of a simple fanatic, relieved, but not concealed, by a pomposity and affectation that are really ludicrous. Much of what M. Hugo writes in epistles to the public is of this character: (witness his appeal for Maxi-

milian to Juarez.*) He seems to think himself not only the primi-
tive and particular apostle of liberty, but the foremost man on all
occasions, and whose sentiments on any public question are of
value, whether he is conversant with it or not. Yet it is this affectation, which would degrade even ordinary talent, and reminds us
of the stage-strut and mouthing of secondrate tragedy-actors, that
is taken, by such asses as *Fledgling*, (though in the text he is not
made to bray) as a proper indication of genius. For example:

"The recent correspondence between Victor Hugo and the young poets of
France . . . . is one of the most graceful and eloquent passages in modern literature. * * * To their expressions of 'boundless admiration' the old poet replied
with a delicacy of compliment, a brilliancy of eloquence, a tenderness of feeling
which showed how well they had called him 'master', and how simply and [yet]
boldly true were their epithets. 'Dear poets, the literary revolution of 1830,
corollary and consequence of the revolution of 1789 [!], is a fact which belongs to
our age. I am the humble soldier of this progress. I fight for revolution under
all its forms — under the literary form as under the social form. I have liberty for
principle, progress for law, the ideal for type.' Our epoch is 'a profound epoch,
against which no reaction is possible. Grand art forms a part in this grand age.
It is its soul. * * We, the old — we have had the combat; you, the young —
you will have the triumph.' Then, in a characteristic generalization, Victor Hugo
declares that 'the *spirit of the* 19*th century* combines the *democratic search for* the
True, with the *eternal law* of the Beautiful', and it directs 'everything toward
this sovereign end, liberty in intelligence, the ideal in art. Literature ought to
be *at once democratic and ideal: democratic for civilization, ideal for the soul.'"
(*N. Y. Times.*)

All of which is as pellucid as plumcake, while at the same time it
is as void of inflation as soap-bubbles.

"In a fine closing sentence," pursues the newspaper youth, "he tells the young
poets, 'I am proud to see my name surrounded by yours. Your names are a
garland of stars'" [of the smallest microscopic magnitude.]

* And more recently his vehement objurgation of those who chose to sentence
and to execute a negro girl of twelve years, who had committed a murder in
Kentucky. The newspapers make him eject froth after this fashion: "Was
there not manhood left in Kentucky to tear out the tongues of the fiends who
pronounced judgment on that girl, and break the arms of those who were base
enough to carry out such a sentence?" Yet M. Hugo has long ceased to be a
schoolboy.

Perhaps he wrote *galaxy*. But it does not matter. Either way, simple or confused, the metaphor is felicitous. If they are the stars, he of course must be the centre of the system; and that he could assert them to be such, and proclaim his own pride to be so garlanded, galaxied, or satellited, is especially illustrative of the "*democratic search for the True,*" — which no one will henceforth doubt has been found by M. Hugo.

15.—P. 435. ACT THE THIRD.] In this Scene, if I shall seem to praise myself, it will be because I copy, as closely as the occasion and the verse will permit, the sentiments expressed by two of the characters in their literary function, and the facts as detailed to one of my brothers by the third.

In taking the liberty I have done in introducing these gentlemen into my piece, I have been guided more by a sense of gratitude than by any other motive. I have so little to be grateful for in all my literary career to my fellows, that I may be allowed to indulge the feeling at the expense of an appearance of egotism, as I certainly have done it to the detriment of my drama.

Begging then pardon of each one, I may say to him safely, if I know myself:

"In freta dum fluvii current, ...
. . . . polus dum sidera pascet,
Semper honos, nomenque tuum, laudesque manebunt,
Quae me cumque vocant terrao."

16.—P. 439. *Because intent   To keep from the light his false argument.*]

Who shames a scribbler? break one cobweb through,
He spins the slight, self-pleasing thread anew:
Destroy his fib, or sophistry, in vain,
The creature 's at his dirty work again. POPE. *Prol. to Sat.*

Just as this 3d Act was passing through the hands of the compositor, I learned that the *Round Table* had, with inconceivable effrontery — no, it was the *Round Table* — had, with characteristic effrontery, dared to talk thus of *Bianca* — of *Bianca Capello*, which I have placed next to *Virginia* in the collective volume of dramas, — *Bianca*, which, however faulty, is full of incident, action and passion, and conspicuous for stage-effect, but whose "plot" is its weakest point, and whose "language and ideas" this sciolist, who cannot write grammatically and has no sentiment but for the commonplace and routine of his trade, condemns by commendation. The emphasizing by capitals and italics is my own.

"There is the *same tiresome prolixity of dialogue*, the *same* PECULIAR WOODENNESS IN THE PERSONAGES of the drama, the *same* FRIGIDITY OF IMAGINATION we before remarked as *characteristic of the author*, but also, it is fair to add [delightful candor !], a symmetry of plot and, *in the main*, a correctness of language and ideas which are his chief virtues. The play is founded on an *episode in the* romantic *history* of Bianca Capello, who, etc." [It happens to be her entire history. Did he really know what is an "episode ?"] "She died in 1587, at *Poggio* [Did she ? It would be as correct to say, The ducal palace was *at Pitti*. She died in the Villa del Poggio *at Caiano*, as he was taught in the drama, as well as in the "Appendices" from which alone the dunce has borrowed all his information] within *a few minutes* of her husband, [that is the play, not history, which the ignorant is affecting to talk after. The briefest interval assigned by historians is *fifteen hours*] both having been taken suddenly ill after a dinner *at* which the grand duke's brother, Cardinal Ferdinand, *participated*." [*Participated at* is good. Here is a smatterer, who pretends to find correctness (I beg pardon, *correctness in the main*) in my language, yet cannot write an article, occupying in its whole extent about half a column of his miscellany, without making three capital mistakes in his own ; for when he says, in the title of the book, "Being *a* completion of the First volume, &c.", he wrote what I did not. Had I so chosen to phrase the title, I should have said "*the* completion ; " but it is really printed "Being *in* completion."] "The cardinal was suspected of having poisoned them, a view which Mr. Osborn adopts, making the motive consist *in his unrequited love for Bianca*." Etc., etc. [Mr. Osborn never made any such thing. He is not a fool, though his cacocritic may be half-a-dozen. But this assertion must be deliberate, therefore wilful, misrepresentation, — like that of the *Nation* when it said I made Judas sell his Master to buy Mary Magdalene bread and butter. The Cardinal, blinded by revenge ·for a supposed injury, the most poignant that could be offered to a man of his temper as well as of his position, permits Malocuor, the inventor of that simulated wrong, to poison both the Duke and Bianca in order to further his the Cardinal's long-brooded ambition. A reader of nature, — which is not either the *Round Table's* waiter or the old woman of the *Nation*, — knows well that it is often these added stings that give the final impulsion to some vicious passion, and prompt to a sudden and violent accomplishment what has been the meditated purpose of years.]

Let us return to the criticism (so to call it). " Prolixity of dialogue " is hardly reconcileable with " symmetry of plot " and " correctness of language and ideas." The dramatist who exhibits these striking merits could not easily commit a fault which can exist only with one who is ignorant of the requirements of dramatic writing. *Symmetry of plot*, if I understand the phrase, implies strict unity of action, and therefore the exclusion of everything that would impede, or even be unnecessary to, that action. Upon this principle, I may be suffered to assert, are all my dramas founded,* and therefore I shall be found to set aside all the useless, awkward, and unnatural train of confidants, and persons whose whole business in a play is to talk, whether wit or wisdom, and whose intervention does not promote one step the evolution of the plot or the approach

* I must be forgiven, if, with considerable hesitation, I venture to append from *Ernestin* (published 1858), the following passage, which I am willing should furnish the standard whereby my dramas are to be measured, although in fact it had reference only to *Virginia*.

. . . . "for the same spirit of truth which guided Ernestin in all things else made him shrink, as at sin, from any violation of probability in the plot, shaped his characters with consistency and exactness, and rendered impossible a want of nature in the dialogue ; while the energy, impetuosity, and fire of his disposition, which in everything he undertook was ever driving him to the end by the straightest and shortest road and without abatement of speed, saved him from irrelevance of incident and superfluousness of persons, shut out all narrative that was not unavoidable, and made his action and his style rapid, vehement, and nervous." p. 348.

This, it may be thought, is high self-praise. But, looking down the not dim vista of the future, and seeing what I there see in its far horizon, the single star that never sets on my grave, I do not fear to write it, and boldly challenge for it the exactest scrutiny.

of the catastrophe. And it is on this account I have said above, that the 3d Act, though introduced with a particular design, spoils the present piece. Having too, I well may claim, an absolute devotion to Nature, sacrificing all needless description, all poetical adornment, where contrary to her requirements, how is it possible that my dialogue should be prolix? Besides, the *Table* knows very well, or there is another point deficient in its qualifications, that in every play extensive mutilations are made in the dialogue to fit it for the Stage.* But the reader shall judge for himself. Bound up in this volume, is the *Montanini*, a drama fitted for performance. If I shall be found to have uttered there any five lines in succession that could have been spared, I will admit the Table-man is less reckless of his assertions in one particular than he appears to be in all.†

For the "peculiar woodenness in the personages": where the

---

* *Vide passim* Inchbald's British Theatre.—I have indicated, myself, some of the abbreviations to be made in my own dramas.

† In the favorite tragedy of *Hamlet*, which has twenty-two interlocutors, great and small, I make out 3482 verses, of all kinds, counting among them the lines of prose dialogue, each of which contains rather more word-matter than a full iambic verse. In *Virginia*, which has twenty interlocutors, whereof sixteen have, perfectly distinctive characters, there are 1690 verses, 31 of which are marked "to be omitted" in the representation. Deducting these, there are but 1659 verses. Thus Shakspeare's *Hamlet* has 1823 verses, or actually one-half, more of dialogue than *Virginia!* Nay, *Bianca Capello*, which covers a period of many years (being a "romantic" drama) and has thirty-three speakers, great and small, contains but 2524 verses all told, or, deducting those marked *to be omitted* (98 in number,) 2426 verses, being 1056 (or nearly one-third) less than in *Hamlet.*

So much for the integrity of this —— Poh! where the deliberate misrepresentation, the crafty mutilation and suppression, the hypocritical depreciation, are so prominent characteristics of all the *Round Table's* notices, beginning with that of *Virginia*, it is but a small matter to find it thus demonstrably false-spoken. The reader will however understand that were my books not kept from circulation, nay *virtually suppressed*, by the malignant calumnies of such mean pretenders, I should not extend to them the honor of an argument, and the *School for Critics* would not take the place of pieces which, like the *Montanini*, do something more than furnish amusement.

proud, yet hypocritical and subtle *Cardinal*, the crafty, double-deal-
ing and perfidious *Malocuore*, the grave, dignified, sensible and honorable *Sennuccio*, the impulsive yet gallant *Bonaventuri*, and Bianca
herself, tender, yet spirited and high-minded, are prominent,— where
even the very *Assassins* have each his distinctive character, and
there is no one without attribute save *Donna Virginia*, who is pur-
posely made so, and is so indicated in the text, — where these and
others are the persons represented, the man who could dare say that
must be either ignorant of his trade — I beg pardon, he is perfectly
master of his trade — ignorant, then, of true criticism, or a wilful
falsifier. Let him be either or both. Probably as both he is useful
in a journal which, according to its own modest and truthful account
of itself in its "*spontaneous* growth," "has labored vigorously for
national literature" and has been "pronounced to be the Ablest Publication of its Class in the United States."* I venture the assertion,
without any hesitancy (because I speak after due comparison), that,
whatever the defects of my pieces, there are not, in the whole range
of dramatic writing from Æschylus down, any series of *characters*
that are better discriminated, more life-like, and more true to nature
than my own.

For the "frigidity of imagination", I have said enough in the 3d
Act of this drama, — p. 436, lines 4–7, and p. 438, ll. 12–18. The
fool or malignant who ventured on that false ascription would, were
his censure conscientious, exclude Schiller, Alfieri, Corneille from
the Pantheon of dramatic poets and put Bedlam Swinburne in its
principal niche. It is the old story. Pope, who, aiming at "correctness," had sense for his lodestar and reason for his monitor, is

---

* One thing is certain. Either the writer of that article is a born fool, or he is
a parcel-educated dullard. I had a brief acquaintance with the late Edgar A. Poe.
On one occasion, when I was speaking of the unpopularity of my works, he said to
me : "We authors, Mr. Osborn, have opinions of our own, and they are in general
very different from those that are retailed to the public by reviewers." Such is
my consolation.

denied by such men the spirit of a poet: the genuine bards are those
alone who give rein to their hippogriff and gallop up and down the
poetical heaven just as the ungovernable mongrel may choose to bear
them. The first principle of good writing is perspicuity. He whose
"imagination" sees clearly will paint clearly, and his words, like
the colors and the tones of a true painter, will not be of the rainbow,
nor of the cloud, but pure, distinct, harmonious; his light and shadow,
though magical in their attraction, will be nature's own, and his design, while free of harshness, in no part vague. The lessons of criticism seem to be excluded from our schools, or to be forgotten. Yet
the principles of true art are the same as they were a hundred years
ago, and will be the same forever, for they are founded on nature
and reason only. Who are the poets that are still preferred? For
one who reads, or better, who has redd Lycophron, there are ten
thousand who joy in Homer still. How is it then, that that which
is so much admired in the latter, his simplicity and distinctness,
should allow of admiration for the glittering fustian of a Talfourd or
the unintelligible jumble of a Swinburne? But such writers are not
really admired, and are never understood. It argues perspicacity,
to pretend to understand them. *Omne ignotum pro mirifico:* what is
not intelligible is taken to be wonderful. In the words of my own
text (let me be permitted to repeat them:)

> For fustian maintains *a name's* illusion
> With man, who is dazzled by word-confusion,
> And finds magnificent and grand
> All that his noddle can't understand,
> And weighty the thoughts from whose tangled skeins
> He fails to draw a conclusion.

Frigidity of imagination, or of anything else, in *me!* —— But the
impertinent did not believe, and never even thought it. It was a
tumid phrase of abusive hemi-criticism, and he used its sound, as
fustianists and magpies do, without a meaning. But when I say,
that to have used it shows he has frigidity of heart and arctic iciness

of conscience, I speak thoughtfully, and mean (with allowance for the stilted language I mimic but to mock) precisely what I say.*

That the reader might know what these creatures are, and that the future may have no trouble to unearth them, I have taken these pains to notice what would otherwise be speedily forgotten. The day will come when the malignant, envious and perhaps revengeful author of that short-sighted article will hide his head for having ejected it on such a tragedy as *Bianca*, as the gentlemen I have ventured to introduce in the present piece as the interlocutors of Act III. will take honor to themselves that they had the sense to feel, the taste and culture to understand, and the conscience to express their judgment and their feeling, in the case of all these dramas, which not ten thousand fools and maliguants can put down, and which shall take their place in my country's literature in defiance of the neglect of her men of real talent and the studied slight of her fifteen-penny criticasters. Living but for truth, as perhaps I shall die for it, one great desire of my life is to represent as they are these parasites on the fair growth of literature, to show them in their actual deformity, their individual insignificance and yet their aggregate noxiousness. — Let me annex but one remark:

If anything could increase my disgust, or add to the turpitude of the pretentious sheet thus noticed, it is that in the leading article of this very Number, it lends its influence to promote the election, to the Presidency of this great republic, of a man who was a traitor to its unity, and not only the abettor of treason, but who had the baseness to address in friendly terms the horrible wretches whose hands were scarcely dry of the innocent blood with which they had sprinkled the ashes of incendiarism and dyed of a more revolting hue the crime

---

* I beg leave to refer to a subnote " (4) " in the 3d Appendix to *Bianca*. The melancholy avowal there made would have moved any but the " frigid " nature I expose to scorn. Yet the heartless blockhead culled out of it an allusion (*After my death, when my countrymen may condescend to read these dramas,*) wherewith to make a gnat's sting of the last of his Lilliputian arrows.

22*

of burglary. But why should I be disgusted? It was meet that the false-tongued journal, which in envy, malice, or in downright ignorance, could lend itself to the overthrow of the temple of true art, should look with complacency on treason, and find no danger to the republic in the advocates or apologists of rebellion and the demagogism that would truckle to the worst passions of a foreign-born mob.

17.—P. 440. *For he took the pains both pieces to cite In a note to his story of* Alice.] *Hinc illae lacrymae.* Had I kissed the rod, I might have counted more sugarplums both for Alice and for Bianca. But the temptation to expose the ignorance, the self-assurance, the flippant impertinence, the hypocrisy, the mendacity, of these animated fungi of literature, was too mighty to resist. So I succumbed, without a permit from Doolady.

18.— P. 442. *Val Jean in the Misérables, — Who, liken'd to Christ in the strife for good* —] This is not my comparison. The more reverent reader will please hold M. Hugo responsible.

19.—P. 447. *Like Ferdinand Mendez Pinto Dixon Who found,* etc.] Malice is contagious. Inoculated with the virus of Mr. Hepworth Dixon's slanders, the *Vie Parisienne*, which the correspondent of the *N. Y. Times* (whence I take the translation) says is an able weekly paper circulating among the better classes of Paris, has the audacity to talk as follows:

" In conclusion, I hardly dare to speak of a certain trait of American manners, it is so delicate ; but I am going to risk it. It appears that there is *a* house at New York, tolerated by the *Government* [!], where they satisfy the wishes of married ladies who do not care for the joys of maternity. A lady, in making her morning calls, tells her friends that on a certain day she had been to the house in question, with as much indifference as if it had been a work of charity. Young ladies are also taken into this house to board, who — but I stop, and for a good cause. When one reflects that an act which carries the people who commit it *so far away from France* [!] appears quite natural in America, he cannot but have a strange opinion of *universal* morality." *July* 30, 1867.

But for the atrocious advertisements which abound in the New-York newspapers, iu none more than iu the *N. Y. Times* itself, it is easy to see that such a wicked absurdity, wherein combine the ignorance, the malice, and the self-conceit, that distinguish in literary matters the " ingehions gentlemen " of the *Round Table*, could never have been concocted. But if not purely the invention of the writers in either case, they have been the victims of a well-known dangerous humor among our people, — that of bantering supercilious strangers, and stuffing their ears with all sorts of libels against themselves. This has been recognized by all of us as practiced on all the note-taking travelers, beginning with Mrs. Trollope and including the cockney Dickens.

I may add, that the most impertinent of the transgressions of these Munchausens is their pretence of describing the most refined society among us as if they were familiar with it, whereas I have never been able to discover that they were in it at all; not at least in New York.

20.—P. 449. *Save one divine article Of which not a particle Shall be lost to the last of the Yankees begotten.*] See above, Note 8, where it will be found preserved, like the fly in amber.

21.—P. 453. — skedaddled —] See next note.

22.—P. 459. — vamos'd the ranch !] A mongrel cant phrase prevalent in the South-west. *Vamos* is the Spanish for *Allons ! Come !* and *ranche* is a corruption of *runcho*, or *rancheria*, which in the Mexican-Spanish of California appears to be used to signify a *farm*, although in the Castilian application of the word (*mess*, or *mess-room*) the composition is intelligible. The phrase is therefore equivalent to the kindred elegancies, *absquatulated* — " skedaddled " — and the English, as well as American, "cut stick." All of which niceties we gather from the newspapers, if they teach us nothing else; and for which, as they are characteristic of our hero S. M., and his congeners, let us be thankful.

23.—P. 462.   *But dotes on Walt Whitman's batrachian fire —*]

"Walt Whitman's 'Carol of Harvest, for 1867,' is a very unequal production. The opening stanzas are *overflowing with poetic feeling*, and their *rythm is sweet and musical.   How tender is the pathos of these lines:*

*   *   *   *

Pass—pass, ye proud brigades!
So handsome, dress'd in blue—with your tramping, sinewy legs;

*   *   *   *

Pass; — then rattle, drums, again!
Scream, you steamers on the river, out of whistles loud and shrill, your salutes!
For an army heaves in sight—O another gathering army!
Swarming, trailing on the rear—O you dread accruing army!
O you regiments so piteous, with your mortal diarrhœa! with your fevers!
O my land's maimed darlings! with the plenteous bloody bandage and the crutch!
Lo! your pallid army follow'd!

But on these days of brightness,
On the far-stretching beauteous landscape, the roads and lanes, the high-piled
     farm-wagons, and the fruits and barns,
Shall the dead intrude?

*   *   *   *   *

Melt, melt away, ye armies! disperse, ye blue-clad soldiers!
Resolve ye back again—give up, for good, your deadly arms;
Other the arms, the fields henceforth for you, or South or North, or East or West,
With saner war — sweet wars — life-giving wars.

"But the following passage" (says the criticaster tenderly) . . . "*reads more like* an extract from an agricultural report than poetry:

*   *   *

The engines, thrashers of grain, and cleaners of grain, well separating the straw,
The power-hoes for corn fields — the nimble work of the patent pitchfork;
Beholdest the newer saw-mill, the cotton-gin, and the rice-cleanser."
— *N. Y. Times*, Aug. 26, 1867.

After that, the honest and capable criticizer notices some of Mr. Tilton's always rythmical verses, and says, "Such verses might be written *by the yard,* and *kept on hand to be cut into pieces* of right [the right] length to fill out a page." Where it will be seen that the ignoramus has uttered what, barring its bad English, might be reasonably applied to Mr. Whitman's *measures.*

24.—P. 466. — *at Willis'.*] Almack's.

25.—P. 482. *He may rank with New England's best.*] Some persons may think this is not paying him a very great compliment. However that may be, it is a just one. But to pick out the child's trifle, and pass over all the well melodized and often nervous poems that precede it, was quite after the fashion of newspaper and magazine witlings, where they have a personal animosity, and is notably *Fledgling.*

26.—P. 485. " *Hanging to dry.*"] Of so brief a quotation, it is not always easy to trace the source, and consequently to explain the allusion. We are able to do this in the present case, only by going to the familiar associations of the *Hotchpot Cryer.* Deadhead had probably in' the cleanly chambers of his memory one of those exhilarating volumes — *Fescennini versus,* which are kept under the tables of the market peddlers and sold with great mystery to schoolboys and servant-maids.

END OF THE FOURTH VOLUME.

www.ingramcontent.com/pod-product-compliance
Lightning Source LLC
Chambersburg PA
CBHW031419020726
47499CB00005B/1504